DORA: a headcase

Lidia Yuknavitch is the author of the novels *The Book of Joan*, *The Small Backs of Children* and *Dora: A Headcase*. Her highly acclaimed memoir, *The Chronology of Water*, was a finalist for a PEN Center USA award for Creative Non-fiction and winner of a PNBA Award and the Oregon Book Awards' Readers' Choice. Her TED talk, 'The Beauty of Being a Misfit', has been watched over two million times. Lidia teaches in Oregon, where she lives with her husband and their son. She is a very good swimmer.

@LidiaYuknavitch | lidiayuknavitch.net

DORA:
a headcase

LIDIA YUKNAVITCH

CANONGATE

First published in Great Britain in 2019 by Canongate Books Ltd,
14 High Street, Edinburgh EH1 1TE

canongate.co.uk

1

First published in the United States by Hawthorne Books & Literary
Arts, 2201 Northeast 23rd Avenue, 3rd Floor, Portland, Oregon 97212

British Library Cataloguing-in-Publication Data
A catalogue record for this book is available on
request from the British Library

ISBN 978 1 78689 332 1

Printed and bound in Great Britain by
Clays Ltd, Elcograf S.p.A.

Crisis as Content:
An Introduction

LEAVE IT TO LIDIA YUKNAVITCH TO TAKE US ALL TO THE next level.

It wasn't that many years ago that rich people could get gussied up, wearing pearls and silver-buckled shoes, coats trimmed in ermine, diamond tiaras and velvet gloves, and thus attired trot through lunatic asylums to watch the resident nutcases masturbate and eat feces. Such a bother, for the rich sane people, all that trotting, I mean. Nowadays, we simply recline on the sofa at home, sipping from our goblets of pinot noir. True, we're forced to peel our own jumbo shrimp, but that's the worst of it. Otherwise, we ogle the usual line-up of basket cases: There's the compulsive hoarder, buried in heaps of squalid garbage and poo-sodden adult diapers. There's the staggering, puke-glazed drunk or pill popper. There's the always-entertaining sexual compulsive – that constantly jerking off, pussy paddling freak show. And there's the obese food-gobbling blimp.

The biggest difference between our modern loony bin slumming and the more ancient practice is that these days we don't have to smell the mess. It's still an exhibition, but today we can observe it from the comfort of our living rooms. Yes, because now the crazies are televised. It's "crises as commodity," or – as I like to call it – "Thera-tainment." Oh, the titles of the programs change, but the die is cast. The shows are called *Intervention* or *Hoarders* or *Too Fat for Fifteen* or *Bad Sex*. And the people appearing on them seem to do so because they have no private options left. Here are the same folks who'd be condemned to the public loony bin or the workhouse of an earlier century. The indigent town drunks or village idiots or neighborhood dirty old men.

Each television show is structured in three dramatic acts. In the first, we witness the vibrant, promising child. There are always baby pictures dredged up, primary school portraits of smiling kids wearing braces on their teeth. In the second act we see what this innocent tyke has become: a home-bound recluse, a bloated pig, a drooling junky, or a skulking porn addict. And in the third act the object of our voyeuristic gaze is offered stern redemption. In fact the entire show is marketed as a redemptive process. We're only here to help. It's with a sincere mask of empathy that we look down on these poor, troubled souls. In this final act, mental health professionals enter to teach coping skills and offer alternative methods of impulse control. It would all be so healthy and productive ... except for the fact that the junkies are wired with microphones; everyone's lower back has the square, tell-tale bulge of a mic pack hidden under his or her clothes. The fatties are gorging on fried chicken, sweating under bright camera lights. And always, unseen, is a crew of people staging every shot.

Worth mentioning here is how all this fuss undermines our concept of aberrant, self-destructive behavior as an illness. Watching *Intervention* or *Hoarders*, the viewer can't help but wonder if it's not all a performance: fake symptoms met with fake therapy and resulting in a fake recovery. Here's apparent proof that the mentally disturbed are, as we've always suspected, simply pretending in order to get more attention.

But, golly gee whiz, it's all so ... captivating. Really, there but for the grace of God go you and me. Without health insurance, that would be us parading our dirty psychiatric laundry to Dr. Phil and Dr. Laura, giving good Thera-tainment value in exchange for their scant advice. Plus a miserly ration of their tough love.

Most often the object's ultimate fate is revealed with a single-card message. It's a sentence or two presented in "reverse" type, white letters on a field of absolute black. Either the stricken sinner accepts the new teaching or they reject it. They live or die. Black or white. All or nothing. And most weeks, the fatty or junky or perv is saved. Hallelujah. But every so often ... the meth-tooting zombie or ranting shut-in dies in the noxious bed of his or her own making.

It always was a kind of slumming: the sane descending to observe the insane, people with money and power staring at those without. It's best not to mention the implied moral lessons about gluttony, lust, greed, and sloth pushed to their extreme, albeit so-deserved, fates. But it does suggest the Saved laying pitying eyes upon the Damned. In the same way we currently trawl cable channels for these train wrecks, no doubt the angels of Heaven will enjoy their eternity all the more because they'll be granted the occasional stroll among those suffering in Hell.

What's not to love? That's Thera-tainment. It offers us a sense of superiority, comfort, catharsis. Each episode is less a melodrama than a cautionary tale or sermon. And the experts imported – the licensed clinical social workers, household organizers, personal trainers, dieticians, etc. – they're nothing less than evangelical missionaries, these disciples of Freud and Jung and Skinner. On a side note, it's ironic how the same institutions which confined the insane also protected them from such media exploitation. Remember the hue and cry over the Diane Arbus photos taken at Willowbrook? Where once only the rich could afford to pay the bribes or "donations" that gave them access to ogle, now everyone who can afford basic cable can enjoy the pathos.

So-called "reality television," what started as merely observation (think of *An American Family* in the 1970s) and practical jokes (think of *Candid Camera* in the 1950s) was not about fixing people. Not at first. But now under the guise of empowerment, the scientific equivalent of a Billy Sunday tent revival, dozens of them, comes into our homes every week. So where do we go from here? Now that we've recognized the profit and status motives of these doctors, trainers, bullies, what's next?

Leave it to Lidia Yuknavitch to show us.

Turnabout is more than fair play; it's healthy. Perhaps as the weak "ill" subjects are exploited for Thera-tainment, now they'll redirect the public gaze back, onto their "healthy" would-be rescuers. The exhibitors will become the exhibition. Only Lidia Y could see where this zeitgeist was going. In *Dora*, she takes the most classic model of Thera-tainment, personal-crisis-as-content, and she re-imagines it wonderfully reversed.

Imagine if Pat and Bill and Lance Loud had covertly decided to counter-manipulate filmmaker Craig Gilbert and public television. It's easy to see how that would've reunited their unhappy family. Or, imagine if some poor sucker on a New York City sidewalk had slammed a cream pie into the smirking face of Allen Funt. That, that would be empowerment. An observed subject secretly, masterfully controlling the observer; that would demonstrate healthy self-actualization. As usual, Lidia Y is running miles ahead of the popular culture. We can't say she hasn't warned us.

The world of *Dora* is not just possible, it's inevitable. It's revenge as the ultimate therapy.

– CHUCK PALAHNIUK

This book is for every teen who ever got treated like something was wrong with them, when really they were opening the portal for all of us. I made this for you. Also, you are right. The adult world is a Fellini movie.

It is fatal to be a man or woman pure and simple; one must be woman-manly, or man-womanly.

VIRGINIA WOOLF

Nothing has really happened until it has been described.

VIRGINIA WOOLF

I.

MOTHER IS CLEANING THE SPOONS AGAIN. FROM WHERE I sit in the kitchen, I can see the reflection of her trippy-looking head: bulbous skull, stretched-down mouth, eyes that scoop away at the rest of her face. A droop-faced woman. Jeeeez. Just look at her. She's rubbing the holy crap out of those spoons. Poor, silvery utensils.

That's what it felt like to be her kid, too.

I can see the inside out of this city from our lame kitchen window. Everything gray going to blue to black. Seattle streets running for all they are worth. Puny pedestrians. Sheets of rain. I can see the Space Needle. Possibly the dumbest thing ever. Rain life makes the scene out the high-rise condo seem like you are in a dream. I put my hand on the window and watch fog surround my fingers. I take my hand away. There I am. A trace. See-through girl. In a pink terry robe and two-day-old underwear. I want a cigarette.

MOTHER. I SIGH. She will rub the spoons until she wipes herself clean.

I rub my eyes. My face feels smeared.

You know what? Seventeen is no place to be. You want to get out, you want to shake off a self like old dead skin. You want to take how things are and chuck it like a rock. You pierce your face or you tattoo your skin – anything to feel something beyond the numb of home. You invent clothes other people think are

1

garbage. You get high. You meddle with sexuality. You stuff your ears with ear buds blasting music so loud it's beyond hearing; it's just the throb and heat and slam and pound and scream of bodies on the edge of adult. You text your head off. You guerilla film. We live through sound and light – through our technologies. With our parents' zombie life dope arsenal at our fingertips.

I'm not a criminal.

I'm just a daughter. I'm not sick.

I.

Just.

Need.

Out.

I walk into the living room. This room always reminds me of Mr. K. It even smells a little like him. When he first came on to me, Mr. K., the friend of my father's, he had a butterknife in his hand. Who knows why a butterknife. He just did. Just me and him in the living room. Just rain whispering like nuns against the pressure of the walls and windows. He had this butterknife in his hand, and he crossed the carpet to me. He trembled. He put his hand on my hip, then he put his other hand near my collarbone. I had a Pixies T-shirt on with safety pins decorating the neckline. He leaned in and sort of suck-nibbled my neck and he whimpered. He smelled like Old Spice and Altoids.

It was so retro. Like something out of a Lon Chaney movie. It should have been in black and white with dramatic and creepy music in the background. I'd have YouTubed it. What the fuck did he think he was doing? I pulled out my pocketknife. I flipped open the blade. He took a step back, thinking it might be for him, I guess. I held the little blade in the air between us. I menaced him. It cracked me up. Then I drew the blade to my own collarbone above the safety pins and Pixies to the very place he had trembled and whimpered. I held his gaze in mine. Without even looking, I made a little smile on my skin. I could hear him swallow.

I was fourteen.

After that I lost my voice. I knew where my voice was. But I wasn't saying. Though it happened years ago, I can still disappear my voice when I need to.

Somehow my father's gotten it into his head I need a shrink. It's all so perfectly Oedipal. Subconsciously he knows I'm onto him and Mrs. K. Who the fuck wouldn't be? He knows Mr. K.'s got his tent pitched for me, so I must be sick. Send the daughter to a shrink. Wash your hands. Straighten your father tie.

My name is Ida. Or used to be.

I have to pee.

I head for the bathroom. My mother barely notices. Or she does notice, but gives no sign. I go in. I lock the door. I sit down. The piss comes out in a gush; I held it a long time. When you hold it just the right amount of time? You can almost cum from peeing. I consider taking a shower, decide instead to cut my hair. I secure scissors from the drawer. I hold up a big wad; chop goes the hair. I hold up another wad, and another, clipping close to my head. I look hilarious. More and more like Sid Vicious. I make faces in the mirror.

"Ida?"

It's the mother calling my name. I must have been in here a while.

"Ida?" Closer. Who the hell names their kid Ida?

Christ. Knocking on the door.

It's then that my father's razor catches my eye – it's the old-fashioned kind for some reason. The kind you unscrew and put a REAL blade in. It's a goddamn antique, I tell you. From a Merchant Ivory movie or something. But it is cool looking. I'm pretty sure it's called a safety razor. Hilarious. I lock the bathroom door.

"Ida!"

I set to work. I feel like an artist. You must hold a razor like that very delicately. Like a paintbrush. The head is heavy. You must let it glide on surfaces so you don't make a mess of things. It takes thirty strokes. I mean to make a masterpiece. I count them. Blood has never bothered me. It's my favorite color, in fact.

Her little fist peppering the door like a motherpecker.

I'm almost done.

At the crescendo of her pecking I set down the razor and take a long and careful look. Admiring my work. Then I throw open the door shouting, "Voila!"

My mother takes a step back and gasps. Her face goes white. From her free hand, a spoon falls to the floor, slow motion, head over end. My head dripping with blood appears briefly like a little cartoon of me in the falling spoon. The spoon makes a metal clatter when it hits the floor. Her mother gave her that silver set. And her mother before that. What's with all the silver? I stare at the idiotic spoon on the floor. Then I pick it up, admire my image, and suck it.

"Ida! What have you done?"

She's staring in horror at my head, completely shaved and nicked-up skull.

I take the spoon out of my mouth and hand it to her.

"I'm a baby bird!" I go. And head for a cigarette.

2.

HERE'S A TIP: WHEN YOU'VE HAD IT UP TO HERE WITH
your parents, develop coughing fits. I'm serious. When they
come at you with their haranguing or advice or expensive wine-
mouthed moralities – start coughing. The more they try to say,
the more you cough – shrug your shoulders and cough your face
off and shake your head like there's nothing you can do about it.

Of course you are likely to get sent to one kind of doctor
or another, but it's a small price to pay. And you'll no doubt run
into the smoky cancer lecture. I think they all go to the same
website to cook up a rant. One of those how to talk to your teenager about fill in the blank.

I'm in the batmobile with my father. He's taking me to the
shrink. Dr. Sig – a nickname I have for my Doctor. Siggy for short.
The batmobile is a custom made Lexus. Black exterior. Tan
leather interior. Tinted windows. I stare at the back of his head.
This is quality time for us, since I hardly ever see him. Dad the
chauffeur. But I think he thinks of this time we share as something else.

My father doesn't want my mother to know he's been balling Mrs. K. for more than two years. He thinks Mother doesn't
know. I think he's a moron. All you have to do is study her behavior. Mother brushes her hair in front of her vanity at night.
Instead of the tubes and powders and brushes meant to paint a
pretty face on a woman, her vanity is covered with small brown
bottles, white bottles, little bitty bottles and bigger ones with lines

and lines of medical instructions that draw her down to them like blush and perfume and lipstick. Adderall and other speedies, Xanax, Vicodin, oxys, morphine, Dramamine, and tranquilizers. They're easy to thieve because she's rendered motherless by about nine p.m. every night. She makes her way through them one at a time in between brushing her hair, humming. It's really creepy. But also weirdly mesmerizing.

If I was a painter I'd paint her face melted with sedation and the ups and downs of a wife gone to zombie.

The batmobile stops at stoplights and makes its stealthy turns. The rain smears the windows and makes passing buildings and cars and people look blurry. The back of my father's head says, "Ida."

I can tell by the sound of his head voice he is going to say something lame. I start with a little "A-hem." A little, gosh, I perhaps have a slight tickle in my throat.

He says, "Ida, this is important. Your mother ... Ida, you've got to stop doing these ... these things to yourself. It's upsetting your mother, what you are doing."

Here he goes. He's revving up his story. He looks at me in the rear view mirror. I surmise he's talking about my new head. He strokes his head subconsciously with one hand. I've learned a lot lately about these little gestures – absentminded actions and facial tics and nervous habits. I stroke my head too. Mirror image. But I know what's coming. He's going to try to talk himself clean some more. He's going to talk right over my knowing, right over my role in his story like the smooth purr of a car engine lying about global warming.

"This thing with your head," his head says, and I let out a hack burst that jumps his shoulders.

"It's important that you take these visits seriously."
  Cough.
"I paid a lot of money to get you the best help."
  Cough cough.
"This doctor is the best money can buy."

6

Coughity cough cough.

"Ida, that's enough—"

I start really wolfing them out now. I start coughing up phlegm and hacking away, drowning him out like I am choking on something – and get this – he starts talking louder. Using a bogus father authority voice.

"Ida," he says all stern, as if using the fake father voice is somehow after all this time going to mean something. "This is no way to behave. You are too old to be acting out like this."

I go to the full-blown tears in your eyes face turning red mode. If I'm too old to be acting out like this, what does that make him?

Coughingcoughingcoughingcoughingcoughing. If I wanted to, I could cough loud enough to shatter the Lexus windows, I could explode the fancy dashboard and eject him from his seat.

"IDA!" he yells.

"You've got to start taking responsibility for your behavior," he yells out full fake dad volume, as we pull up in front of Dr. Sig's office – only I've stopped coughing, so my father's just yelling like an idiot into dead air – his words hanging there between us. He looks at me in the rear view mirror. I shrug. We stare at each other in the little reflective surface. He unlocks the batmobile doors. I open the hermetically sealed father mobile – where his stories of himself glide along roads effortlessly – and exit into rain. As he drives away I close my eyes and put my face up to the sky. The rain is cool on my head and face.

Every Thursday my father delivers me like this.

So he can drive away from what he's made.

3.

I KINDA WONDER IF THE SIG WATCHES HIS CLIENTS
approach from his upper office window. Maybe grabbing at his
crotch like a dirty old man. His office is on the second floor of a
chic Seattle restoration, and it has a long thin window with creepola floor-length drapes. I swear I've seen his beady little peepers
just beside the drapes before. It's hard to tell though from down
on the street. Looking up. If he is looking down today, he's in for
a treat. What with my new head and all. I give myself a head rub
for luck.

I walk toward the entrance of the office building. I stop. I
look up, smile and wave, blow a kiss just in case.

This is my seventh meeting with the Sig. I have learned a
few things, boy howdy. If anyone ever tells you that going to see
a shrink is therapy? Tell them to suck a fart out of your sweet
asshole. It's not therapy. It's epic Greek drama. You gotta study up.
You got to bring game.

Inside the office building, I push the button and the soft
coo of elevator happens. I bet he listens for the coo. I bet he pictures my combat boots when I walk down the hall to his office.
Who can resist red leather docs and teen girl calves?

Lemme lay out the stage for you – the inside of Sig's office,
I mean. First of all, there are way too many Pottery Barn lamps.
Trust me. The 'rents have our condo all decked out in PB and
Restoration crap, so I recognize bouge hell when I see it. Now
picture all those lamps with the lowest wattage bulbs in the

9

world. So that the room isn't really "well lit." It's just sort of end-lessly brownish yellow, everywhere you look. What they call "warm" light. Probably meant to keep all the nutcases calm. More like swamp glow, if you ask me.

Then there is this gigantoid mahogany man-desk. Can we say over-compensating? If there's ever a second flood, the Sig's ready. That thing could carry lots of fucking animals. On the man-desk is an ashtray – so old school – so not PC in our smokeless, faux, eco-friendly workspaces. The Sig? Apparently he's a stogie man. I've seen a half-smoked brown stub.

I think the only place I have ever seen cigars being smoked is in black and white movies and old folks homes. Weird.

OF COURSE the office walls are lined with about a gazillion books, because we wouldn't want anyone to miss his über smarty-pantness or big-brained balloon head, now would we? Some-times he saunters over to the books and – I shit you not – *strokes the spines*. Ew.

What else. Two absurdly expensive-looking Persian rugs, no doubt woven by terrorists, another little table with coffee-maker shit on it, a high camel-backed sofa chair that he sits in when we do our thang, and some bizzaro abstract painting of … a forest? Hard to tell. The trees would only look like trees if you were tripping. "Art" for over the hill rich people.

But the pièce de résistance? The couch. Yep, you heard me. The Sigster has a giant couch. It stretches out for client nuts as the only option – all Italian brushed leather.

"Dude, what's up with the couch? I gotta sit on that thing?" was my first commentary. He went off on some crap about reflexology – some batshit theory about how people's sub-consciouses are more easily released when they are in reclined positions.

"Isn't it also easier to see up girl skirts?" I went.

"That is not the matter at hand," became his regular defense. Man if I had a Vicodin for every time he's said that to me … I could fill one of my mom's prescription bottles.

You might say we set the rules in that first exchange. Like I say, I've learned a lot about our little dialogues since we began. Now I come prepared.

I never travel in the world defenseless. First off, I wear a Dora the Explorer purse everywhere I go. You know, from kid TV? It's pink and shiny and hangs across my chest on a long-frayed string. I got it as a kid, but I've made modifications since childhood. Two safety pins where my little cartoon chica's eyes used to be. And I gave her a blow-up doll's mouth with a red Sharpie. And I painted a little gun for a hand. Sweet, really. That dumbass little blue monkey that hangs around with her though – I had to make him into a death skeleton.

Inside my Dora purse I don't have mascara or lip gloss or gum. I don't have breath mints or tampons or a joint. I don't have candy or condoms. What I have, is my beloved Zoom H4n audio recorder. At all times. Everywhere.

Especially here.

I knock.

He opens the door.

"Ida," he goes.

"Sig," I go. How it's never occurred to these folks how AWK-WARD the fake-o greetings are is beyond me. Hi. It's me. Your 4:00 nutter. Hello, won't you come in and let me explore your genitals by pretending to talk about your family origins. What a load of crap.

Once I'm in, I'm *in*. This place is mine. I'll tell you why later. It's me against him. The opening moves are important. I turn to look at him. I smile the smile of a girl on the cusp of things. Whaddya got for me today, Siggy. Gimme your best shot.

He stares at me. "I see you've … changed … your hair," is all he's got. Christ. Child's play.

I twirl around with great drama. Then I stand extra upright. I whip my hand up to my head and jut my chin out. He looks alarmed. Like I might attack him. Instead, I violently salute him, click my heels together, look slightly above his sad little pad of gray hair, and shout, "Herr Doktor!"

Fuck yeah.

Smoked him speechless.

4.

SOMETIMES HE'S SUCH A CHODE.

I'm serious.

I mean sometimes when I hit playback I just have to roll my eyes and think, what happens to these graying guys? These middle-aged meat sacks? Do their brains atrophy like their ball-sacks do? I mean, they've got Viagra for the nuts issue, what do they take for the fucking brain sag? By the way, I've taken Viagra, and though it's true that if you are a girl it will drop your blood pressure to faint on the floor if you aren't paying attention, it can make your cum job do loop de loops. They don't like to tell women that. Typical. The shit they're coming up with for women pales in comparison. Let's just say no funding's going down that hole.

Anyway, get a load of this:

"I believe the early disgust you experienced in the first sexual instance, when he tried to kiss you at fourteen, came about as a symptom of repression in the erotogenic oral zone, which, as you yourself related, had been overstimulated in your infancy from thumbsucking."

Oh, but wait, it gets even better:

"The kiss then stimulated disgust not only because it triggered a moment of sexual excitement – but because the pressure of his erect member probably led to an analogous change in your clitoris – in this embrace, you simultaneously desired and feared the male member, and displaced those emotions orally."

Did you fucking hear that? Wait. It's too too good. Lemme play it again.

See?

Pure chode.

I play it and play it. In Marlene's loft apartment, overlooking Fisherman's Terminal Dumbasses on ferries in the distance. Tourists hoping someone will throw a fish at them at the market, or sell them coffee and chocolates. I turn the sound all the way up and play back again. The first recording I tried my iPhone, got home and immediately realized I needed an upgrade. It sounded like crap. Now I carry my beloved Zoom H4n – you can capture four-track stereo recording anywhere. Even from inside a Dora the Explorer purse. If you leave enough zipper room to clear its coaxial mic.

To me, no matter what words he is saying, Sig's voice sounds soft and raspy, except when he wants to sound important. Then he tightens his throat and aims his chin down toward his clavicle shooting for some über smarty guy he must have been in his past. When he does that chin down thing? Kind of he looks like he needs to burp. But with very stern eyebrow action.

Marlene is making bacon. She laughs and laughs – a deep throaty Rwandan one. You heard me. I've got that laugh recorded. If you've never heard a Rwandan laugh, you are missing something mega-cool.

I say, "I've never heard a laugh so deep."

She says, "It is my dark continent. It lives in my belly!"

Isn't that cool? I have no idea what the fuck that means, but isn't it cool?

"What does that even mean?" I ask.

Again the laugh. I record it.

"It is a statement made by history. I had to eat it, and now it is in my belly." She laughs and I laugh too, my laugh riding hers like a girl on a pony.

"Can you teach me to laugh like that?" She just smiles. All I know about Rwanda is words like genocide and Tutsis and

14

Hutus. Piles of skulls and bones. From TV. That's why I say her laugh has something in it. Mega.

With her back to me, she says, "Someday, you will learn to laugh with your whole life."

Bacon sizzles and pops. I can smell pig heating up.

This is where I spend most afternoons and evenings – in Marlene's loft, reading her shelves and shelves of books from a gazillion years ago – books that drip sex from the annals of history. They are the only books she owns. Like an antique sexuality library. You'd be amazed how much cooler old books are than new ones. Take Havelock Ellis. *Sexual Inversion*. 1897. Man that Havie was one weird and zany guy. My favorite of his though is *Love and Pain: The Sexual Impulse in Women*. 1903. Why can't I find any books like this written by non-dead folks?

Then there's the collected pamphlets of Abner Kneeland – the last guy to be tried for blasphemy in America. Apparently Mr. Christian got a little loose with his sex talk. Started some weird utopian cult called The Freethinkers society. Right next to that is a buddy of his – Charles Knowlton. *The Fruits of Philosophy, or the Private Companion of Young Married People*. 1832. This guy was prosecuted a bunch of times. The book was about birth control. Figures. Next to that, the collected speeches of Victoria Woodhull, including "The Scare-crows of Sexual Slavery" (1873). Very Emma Goldman. Of course Emma is up there too, along with photography and art and medical and philosophy books. And all manner of pornology – that's what Marlene calls it – as long as it was published before 1945. And everything ever written by the Marquis de Sade.

One word for you. *Justine*.

With her big man hands Marlene makes bacon. With big man calves she struts around the kitchen in a midnight blue silk robe and platinum wig and alligator pumps. She bends and presents me with a plate of bacon, her lips red as a Coca-Cola can, her eyes circled with kohl. With her Adam's apple bobbing she says, as deeply and sweetly as the real Marlene, "Won't you have some Schwein, Liebchen?" Her skin so dark I want to lick it. If I was ever gonna choose a mother, this would be her. Chocolate Madonna.

I fill my mouth with sizzled pig. Possibly my favorite food ever.

Marlene is a manwoman. I first met Marlene at the Wet Spot below Queen Anne Hill. Before it went porno they had wonderful horrible punk band shows. Marlene was at the door taking the benjamins. Since no alcohol was sold or served, we could all get in – buncha whacked-out kids with their parents' pharmaceuticals in their pants and flasks in their underwear. We danced so hard every night we baptized ourselves in bruise. Alongside punkers and bikers and strange angry bald guys – no doubt neo-Nazis or some shit. Marlene was always reading books from inside her little money booth, so one night I went in there and we just really hit it off. She was looking at a book of erotic photos from like before 1900 or something. The Charlotte Baker series by Gustave Rejlander. They were weirdly creepy. I adored her immediately.

She sits across from me and pours herself a scotch. Pours me one as well. I play back once more. This time I catch a bit with my own voice in it:

"Yeah? Well I once saw my father getting sucked off by Mrs. K. They were in his study. The door was ajar. Saw him pop his cork, basically. She had her skirt up over her big, white, adorable ass. How's that for family romance?"

Then Dr. Sig's voice goes, "Yes, your witnessing your father's desire satisfied orally is of great consequence in your narrative."

I hear myself go, "Look, Doc. It's not rocket science. It's a fucking blowjob."

My stomach twists. I hate the sound of my voice. "I think he thinks I'm a pussy," I say to Marlene. Stuffing what's left of my bacon into my mouth.

Holding her piece of bacon between her long-nailed

fingertips and taking a tantalizing tiny nibble at a time, Marlene says, "How so?"

"Well I think he thinks I'm actually there for …" I fill my mouth. I hit rewind. I look at the hardwood floor.

"For what, Lamskotelet?" Marlene takes a sip and I can see she's savoring the bacon and scotch in her mouth before.

She.

Swallows.

This is among her many pet names for me. Lamskotelet. Lambchop. In German. Marlene's father and grandfather were German. I've learned things you never hear at school about the history of Rwanda. Lamskotelet. I grin like a girl with a mouthful of bacon. I talk with my mouth full. "Sometimes I think he thinks I'm a moron. That I'm a confused depressed little second wave EMO girl. That I'm there at these appointments … you know, for real."

Marlene claps her bacon hands with blue-lacquered nails and throws her head back and laughs the laugh. She suddenly rips off her platinum and tosses it across the room. The little black-webbed hairnet exposed and weirdly glorious.

"I have the perfect books for you today!" she announces, her hands clasped in front of her face like Christmas, and she sashays away to the shelves.

I busy myself rewinding to a different moment in the day's recording. Hoping for a humdinger. Hoping to drown out my own voice.

I'm making a mix.

Dr. Sig's voice with cut-ins of Bowie, Lou Reed, Black Flag, Richard Hell, the Adverts, X, and this hilarious bit with Elliott Smith up against Dr. Sig's discussion of suicidal impulses. If all goes well I'll have a mix ready by the xxx-mass rave at The Kasbah. At full decibel, it oughta be one helluvah show.

When she returns, Marlene has what looks like two one-hundred-year-old at least ten-by-twelve dark red cloth-cover beauts. She hands them to me. They're heavy. Not like books now.

I can feel my biceps while I hold them. My heart races. Nothing is better than these old books in Marlene's loft. Well, almost nothing. I place them on the table. They smell like dirt and old. They look like something before capitalism. Not disposable. Not fast. Nothing about Barnes & Noble. I look down at the titles and screw my face up.

Fisiologia del Dolore. Fisiologia dell'Amore.

"What do they say?" I say.

"*Physiology of Pain.* 1880. And this one," she pets the other as if it is beloved, "*Physiology of,*" she pauses and closes her eyes, "*L o v e .* 1896."

I stare at the author's name and want to eat it with my bacon and scotch: "Mantegazza," I say, shooting for not American-mouthed.

"Mantegazza," Marlene echoes.

My recording sessions, I have to say, I think of as a stroke of pure genius. I have to wonder if any other patients do this. I can't be the only one who has thought of it, can I? And it's just so kick-ass to play back when you get home. Beats the fuck out of television.

Other times though when I'm listening I feel itchy. Like … I don't know. I feel kind of like I get him. I mean like radically. I mean like I can see and feel what he means before he says it. Which makes no sense. Our lives are nothing alike. We're so far from each other we are like illegal aliens to each other's countries. Old man balls. Still. Sometimes it's like his words were already in me.

I pick up the beautiful heavy red books. When I go to put them in my backpack I see greasy thumbprints on the covers. I smile. "Marlene, I'm gonna take a whiz," I say. In the bathroom I sit on the toilet. I pull out the recorder and play back, my own pee another sound layer. Siggy's voice goes:

"Your father has made you ill. You experience your own passions as evil, just as you perceive his to be evil. The punishment for which is illness."

I just sit there drip-drying with my elbows on my knees and my chin in my hands thinking. Yeah. I get that. Way down. My vag spasms a little. Piss shiver.

But when I wipe up I hear him ask the lame-o question of the year: "Do you masturbate, Ida?"

With my erratic bird voice going, "Do you? I mean men your age?" Christ. Had to be quick on the draw on that one. How and when I touch myself is none of his goddamn business. And my twinkle pet information is only available on my terms. I'll use it if and when I need it. Perv.

Then his voice on the H4n goes, "Ida, it is not a condition of our relationship as patient and doctor that we discuss my sexual history. It is your sexual history that has bearing on the content at hand. It is your sexual history that has put you in a difficult position." It's not the soft raspy voice. It's the man he thinks he used to be voice. Deep and clear-throated. Chin down.

Clever bastard. Then I hear me going, "Yeah, but aren't you supposed to also build up some kind of fake Herr Doktor trust shit so I'll tell you all my girl secrets? Transferral or Trans-fickle or Transfuck or something? Why should I tell you jack shit if you aren't holding? What's in it for me?"

God I hate my voice. There's no whole body yet in that voice.

And he goes, "Help. Help is what's in it for you. Do you want to go into your life as an adult coughing and losing your voice? Do you want to move into your future relationships with all of these mixed-up emotions? I can help you straighten it all out. It begins in your dreams."

Sly smug one, he is.

To which I thought the only solid one would be to tilt my head to the side, soften my eyes and mouth, s l o w l y finger my purse in my lap and say, "Are you mad at me or something?"

I shut off the playback. I give myself a once-over in the bathroom mirror. I already have five o'clock shadow on my head. I laugh. Still nothing-girl voice. I open the mirror medicine cabinet. There are all of Marlene's pills. Lined up quite perfectly.

I zoom in on a bottle – pick it up – bring it closer – that's when I see her name. His. Hakizamana Ojo. I put my finger on the words. Possibly the coolest name I have ever touched. Then I pocket the pills. She's got lots of them.

Do I masturbate? You know what? Siggy can suck it. You have to watch out for these little booby traps. You have to stay one step ahead of the game. He's got my father's money on his side. The purse strings. He's got the power to make a story of me that will make or break me. Think about it. If you can't outsmart a middle-aged shrink by the time you are eighteen, how the hell are you going to get through a life?

I thank Marlene for the books and bacon. When I get home I'll go into my bedroom and lock the door. I'll log and capture my newest audio onto my Mac. I've got software. I'm mixing voices.

I consider it my duty to beat Sig's story of me. Like a race. Because baby, on my eighteenth birthday, I'm so fucking outta there.

5.

RAIN FALLS ON MY HEAD. I WALK DOWNTOWN ADMIRING
Seattle's gritty little grime holes – the alleys between galleries.
The backs of brick buildings where dumpsters live. Parking garages
of high-rise businesses. I record sound. If you listen, you can
hear metal on concrete. Or water dripping. Or wind in the urban
spaces.

My cell vibrates the front pocket of my skinny jeans. It's
the posse.

The posse is not "my peers." We are more like a micro-
organism. As in Darwin. I've read Darwin. I stole his book from
the library. I'd party with Darwin.

The posse hooks up. Tonight the textcode is *6NDSTpine-
wear*. You don't know what that means but I do. I'm guessing
drunk hide-and-seek or bra slingshot. One hundred points if you
hit a salesperson in the ass. I get vibrated a few times in quick
succession. Little Teena has Percocet. Ave Maria has Sweet Tooth.
Haven't heard yet from Obsidian. Obsidian. Obsidianobsidian.
Just the word dizzies me. My Obsidian.

I text the posse *VbigD*. Viagra. Marlene's. I walk more. My
head wet.

Vibrate. It's Obsidian. Obsidian has speedies. Like I give a
shit what she's holding. My cell gets hot in my hand. My ears
beat blood.

In the world of the posse, it doesn't matter if you are male or female. Or anything in between. We share drugs. We share bodies. We make art attacks.

Oh and there is no member of the posse that hasn't slept with every other member of the posse.

Well.

Except for me.

I am … I have …

Look. Can we discuss this for just a second? Virgin could mean lots of things. I've never had full blown bang. Sue me. I don't know. I just … let's just say when it comes to the high nasty I go numb. Deaf. Mute. Or I cough. OK, I pass out.

It ain't from lack of trying though.

Take wang for instance.

What's the big deal with wang sex anyway? I've been around lots of wangs. I've seen my father's. Ew. I've sucked Mr. K's. I've seen Little Teena's – which has a thick silver stud in it – I've seen Marlene's – both fully erect and tucked in tight for ladies' nights. That's a lot of dong for a virgin. But getting that dang thing inside me? Makes me go cold. Dead.

OK. It's not just a wang issue.

Fuck it. I don't want to talk about it.

Virgin also means mother of Jesus, doesn't it?

Also a female insect that produces eggs without being fertilized. I googled it. Put that in your pipe and smoke it.

So yeah, I'm a motherfucking virgin. Which pisses me the fuck off. Being angry makes me feel better. I don't know. I just feel better when I'm pissed.

Vibrate. The posse's on the move.

I walk the city. Black backpack black ear buds black hoodie black skinny jeans black leather wristbands FIRE-ENGINE RED SHINY DOCS. I stomp up the hill to the beat of X. Rain barely lands on my head. This pair of jeans always turns me on if I walk uphill just right. Sing it, Exene. Creamy. I stick my hand in my Dora purse. I'm on "record" picking up street sounds. I'm a head and a body and technology. I'm my own walking history.

But not just that. Gimme a V to the I to the R to the G to the I to the N. I hate my twat. I hate my voice. I hate feeling anything about myself. I sprint my ass up to Nordstrom's.

In the underwear department of Nordfuck's there they all are – not standing together, but spread out in various lingerie nooks and crannies. Little Teena, a whole lot of redheaded well-coifed gay boy at 282 pounds. Ave Maria, stringy long blond hair, wrists as thin as tent poles – our bulimic poster child. Got her name because she hits a high note when she cums that makes you believe in saints. And then there is Obsidian. Obsidian with the blackest longest hair in ever falling in lines over her right eye. My desire. I vibrate, but it isn't my cellphone.

Oh, and yours truly. Dora the Explorer. Pathetic virgin with a hot hard one for a girl with the name of a black glass stone.

Obsidian's Native American. On the rez in Coeur d'Alene where she grew up her drunk stepdad beat the crap out of her mom and then came into her bedroom and raped her. Now she wears a knife-sharp shard of obsidian around her neck – tied with black leather. I think she could kill someone with that shard if she had to. Sometimes I wonder if she did. She doesn't say much but her eyes have war in them. It makes me wish I had a horse. A hatchet. War paint.

That's a lie. That's my fantasy of us together – riding across the plains of some country in my head.

So I don't have to think about what a fucking idiotic dysfunctionoid twat I am. V is for virgin. My eyes sting and my throat squeezes and I pinch myself at the thin skin of my neck to snap out of it. I make my way deeper into the Nord. *Suck it up, you pussy*.

In the panty department, the scrawny saleswoman with the shellacked head of blond bats her stupid eyelashes and darts her eyes from one to the other of us. She's so nervous we're going to steal shit she's bunching up the panties she's supposed to be folding for the display. It just makes me feel better to hate her. "Careful of those crotches," I murmur as I brush past her.

Turns out it's drunk hide-and-seek. Little Teena has hidden three fifths of vodka in the store and we have to find them and consume them before some lame-ass mall cop does. If you find one, you drink, then hide it again. Trust me. After the bottles are open it gets easier and easier to find them. Plus you can sprinkle some on clothes to leave a little trail. My mother always said vodka is odorless. But that's bullshit. Explains why she often smells like pickled Estée Lauder. Good clean healthy fun. Kids these days, huh? What? Would you rather we were checking out your internet porn? Or hacking into your email? And by the way, just who are you calling troubled teen, Mr. and Mrs. Pharm zombies?

Obsidian and I find the first bottle stuffed down the Dockers of a neutered male mannequin over in THE MENSWEAR department. We leave his fly open and crawl underneath a big round jeans donut rack and drink. It smells like denim martinis. But inside the jeans world I can also smell her skin. Something between rain and trees. I stare at the side of her face where her hair hangs down. I stare at her so hard my eye twitches. I try to breathe her.

When we've slugged a few shots, Obsidian says, "Where you wanna put the bottle next?"

Since she can't see me through her hair, I say, "Inside you," blushsmiling. My skin itches. I cough. I see stars. She laughs. I wish. Though we've sucked face plenty, and I've gone down on her other mouth like a goddamn gleeful leech, we haven't … I just …

She turns to me so she's facing me and I can't stand looking at her anymore. She closes her eyes and says, "Kiss me, Dora." I try not to headbutt her with the force of my face moving toward hers. I kiss her. I kiss her and kiss her. I try not to bite her lip. She tastes like vodkahoney.

Then it's her lunging at me inside the jeans donut, knocking me down to the Nord floor, it's her lying on top of me and kissing me and I hope I die right that second. Her hair down on my face her skin rain and trees her hips pushing against mine her dagger of black stone hanging down and touching the hollow of my neck. Let her neckrock stab me and kill me. Please let me die like this. I shiver and pant and almost cry.

That's when it happens. Like it always always fucking does. I go numb. My hips, my legs, my crotch. I see starbomblets, then I see gray blotches, then white.

Next it's Obsidian saying, "Dora? Dora? Come back, baby. It's OK. Come on back." Petting my cheek and lifting me up until she's cradling me like a goddamned infant. Fuck. I should just go ahead and suck my thumb.

She rocks me for a while, then pulls back, then we just sit there, neither of us knowing what to say. About me. About my … thing. We slug more vodka. We eat speedies.

After she just sucks in a big sigh of air and turns to me like everything is cool and goes, "So. Where'd we say we'd put it next?" I stuff my shame down my throat. Then farther down. I cough. I laugh. I get pissed. I come back up.

"How about in COSMETICS?" I suggest. "We can chase a couple of those moronic perfume wenches who try to spritz you with scent and christen them with holy water from the rear."

"Excellent plan," she goes, and we're off.

I wish I could punch myself in the face. I shove the me that sucks so far down it's in my pants.

That's about when it happens. Coming down the escalator from one Nord floor to the next we see Little Teena has commandeered the grand piano. He's busy busting out Bach to all the bewildered shoppers. Little Teena just doesn't look very Nordstromy sitting there, with his red hair slicked up in a pompadour, his girth squeezing out between his black leather jacket and the lip of his jeans, gumball-machine rings decorating every single one of his fingers. But it's when he goes from Bach to "Great Balls of Fire" that we attract the attention of the Nordfuck's militia.

"A bottle!" Little Teena yells, holding out one of his bejeweled hands, and I chuck it to him. It's really kinda glorious the way he plays with one hand and reaches Statue of Liberty-like to catch the vodka bottle in the air.

Still playing with one hand, and only pausing to chug vodka, Little Teena gives the place a taste of pure teen homo joy.

Ave Maria begins dancing and hitting random high notes for no particular reason. Her stringy blond hair flying. I start recording big time. Obsidian yells out, "I shop, therefore I am!" every few seconds. It's like I've been saved. From a self. I'm so happypissedhigh I feel like I've been shot out of a rocket into the sky.

I do the only sensible thing. I step out of my Docs. I remove every bit of my clothes (keeping my purse on, of course) and douse myself in vodka. Obsidian immediately begins to lick my arms. Somehow I don't pass out. Some old bag shopper drops her Nords bag and gasps, saying, "Mother of God!" A tight-assed shoe guy walks briskly over but stops at the perimeter, pacing. Then there is a swarm of tan-pantsed guys with little black walkie talkies – some kind of Nordstrom tan-pants team of thugs –

and everyone scatters. Everyone, of course, except me, the lone naked girl. My skin stinging. I suck my bicep. Vodkaskin. Reborn. Angry. Neat.

One of the tan pants grabs a coat off of a nearby rack and puts it around my shoulders. Ha! It's a fucking trenchcoat. I go, "You're gonna regret that next paycheck, ese," but he's already driving me by the shoulders out of the area.

Down and down some kind of service corridor.

Down Dante-like to the bowels of Nordfuck's.

To a little white shoplifters cubicle with a closed-circuit TV mounted on the wall. I'm not the pussy me here. I'm the me who takes action and isn't sorry. I'm Dora. "Wow," I say, "that is some cheap-ass surveillance system you got there. What is that, boys, like 1973?"

They talk at me. But I know the routine. It's no big thing. Besides, I haven't stolen anything, I just made a teen scene. I had the audacity to remove my clothes inside a shopper's clothing empire. But I'm underage, so there you go. I told you, I'm not a criminal. I'm back in the saddle.

They ask me over and over what my name is and I say "Dora." I hold up my purse and wave the little cartoon girl at them and point. They manhandle the Zoom H4n – which is recording four sound layers at a time. Ha. They check my backpack for ID but what kind of moron would carry ID these days? What they do find, however, is the Viagra. The Viagra of Hakizamana Ojo. From Rwanda. Only they can't pronounce it at first. Idiots.

"Who is Haykeezeeman-uh-OJ?" Priceless. I correct their pronunciation. They repeat it back to me. I sneak a peek at the Zoom H4n – yep, there it is on the table, still recording. That's gonna make a nice riff: Who is Hakizamana Ojo? Who is Hakizamana Ojo?

Finally, I shout, "Why, he's my mother!" They look at me skeptically and speak some gibberish into their walkie talkies. "I tell you he's my mother!" I continue to bellow. The party mix recording just kicked up a notch.

Then they pull out my black Pixies hoodie. They eyeball it like it's a dead animal. Whatever. Chumps. Of course they pull out Marlene's book – *Fisiologia dell'Amore* by Mantegazza – and look at it – pretty much how chimps might. They'd best not mess with that. Next they pull out a spoon. They hold it out at me like that means something. I go, "Yeah. It's called a spoon." Then one of them brings it to his nose and sniffs it. Ha. Trust me when I say it's not what he's expecting. I'll tell you later. Then the one guy reaches down and pulls out something tiny. Something I totally forgot was in there. A business card. A psychiatrist's. Dr. Sig's.

"Who is this," they ask and ask. "Have you any relation to this person?"

I look at them and blink as slowly as possible. One of the tan pants has grease on his tan pants' thigh. Probably from lunch. Where do they find these guys? And why do they always have long sideburns? Curious. The pudgier one of the tan pants holds Dr. Sig's card in the air between us. It suddenly seems super obvious what to say.

I smile and stand up, letting the trench coat fall to the floor. I put on my hoodie. Though I remain pantsless.

"That, boys, is my father," I say dreamily. "I think you should call him."

6.

NEEDLESS TO SAY, THE 'RENTS WERE PISSED. ABOUT THE whole Nordfuck's episode.

Father came home in the batmobile and went straight for a scotch – probably to wash the taste of Mrs. K. out of his mouth. Mother put down her spoons for a second and flapped her arms and squawked like a chicken – how I'd made another scene again in public – how I rode home in a cop car – how she can never shop at Nordfuck's again. Father said to her, and I quote, "Calm down. Would you calm down? Give me a minute to decompress from my day before you start claiming the sky is falling." I stood in the hallway. Wished I had popcorn. I love their little dramas. "Ida, go to your room," he said, his voice full of nothing. Ida go to your room? Whoa. Heavy.

To be honest with you I didn't think being "grounded" was around anymore. It's so … retro. Usually I just climb out the condo window onto the fire escape. But tonight I sorta feel … I don't know, home-y.

At home in my room my walls kick ass. Lou Reed. Exene. Siouxsie Sioux. Kurt Cobain. David Bowie. Nico. Did you know Nico was fluent in four languages? That's not what you hear about her. Typical. Marlene told me that. I lie down on my bed. I look at my ceiling. Hoping for a crack that means something.

In my bedroom I write letters on the walls. Hidden underneath the wall posters. With a purple Sharpie. Today I'm writing under Nico.

What I write are Dear Francis Bacon letters. Francis Bacon the painter. You know, the guy who painted the screaming melting pope. Possibly the coolest painter in ever. Why? It's the faces. He makes faces look like they can't hold still. That's so right on. Marlene gave me a giant Francis Bacon book a year ago and I just about peed. That Francis Bacon understood how faces are. For instance. When you get up close to someone to suck face? Their faces look like Francis Bacon paintings. No lie. I so get that. A face that just might smear off or explode. Underneath Nico I write: "Dear Francis Bacon: My face is an I hole."

Basically I'm making a book out of the walls of my bedroom. Something for the spawners to decipher after I'm gone. Some day the spawners will walk across the purple shag carpet and start the process of taking their daughter's posters down for a remodel – my father wants a home office; my mother a fucking crafts room – that's when they'll find my words. I study my handiwork.

Then I pull out the new book Marlene gave me – *Fisiologia dell'Amore*. By Mantegazza. Hope the mall chimps didn't drool on it or anything. I open it.

Yeah. So it's in Italian. But that's not the cool part. The cool part is, just underneath every line, and I mean every single line, there is another line. In pencil. For every line of the book. Translated by Marlene. Who, like Nico, knows four languages. Marlene's lines under all of Mantegazza's lines. Maybe she even rewrote some of it.

The second cool as shit thing is the Mantegazza quote that opens the book. It goes:

> *To the daughters of Eve, that they may teach men that love is not lechery, nor the simony of voluptuousness, but a joy that dwells in the highest and holiest regions of the terrestrial paradise, that they may make it the highest prize of virtue, the most glorious conquest of genius, the first force of human progress.*

I close the book and hold it on top of my chest. Daughters of Eve. Fuck yeah. That's me. I don't think of Eve as a twat that got tricked by a snake. I think Eve was a badass. I think she showed Adam what to do with his dick, and without her, he'd be sticking it in knotholes and goat butts and suckerfish. Without Eve? Adam's just a guy standing around with a dick in his hands. Daughters of Eve. Wicked band name.

And love: *The most glorious conquest of genius. The first force of human progress*. Fucking fuck yeah. I roll over and look at the ceiling. There is a crack in the plaster in the shape of a vag. Seriously. Under the sign of Vag, I feel positively dreamy with Marlene's big book. Me and Obsidian. Obsidian Obsidian Obsidian. Daughters of Eve. I sit up and get the purple Sharpie and write the Mantegazza quote on my bedroom wall. Under Nico. Vibrate. I grab my cell out of my back pocket where it buzzes my butt. "Obsidian?" Nope. It's Marlene.

She goes, "Lamskotelet! How do you find the book?"

"Dreamy. I'm a Daughter of Eve!" She does the deep laugh. Even through a cellphone it's something. "I just started it. It's awesome." We talk for a while and I agree to come over the next day to talk about the book. I lift Nico up again and write "Lamskotelet" in purple Sharpie.

Yep, me jailed in the daughter box writing up a storm. But that's not all I'm doing in the daughter box. I'm listening for family drama. Household electricity. My dad looks a little like Daniel Day-Lewis so it's easy to picture him in some crappy historical drama acting all serious and righteous and crap. My mom looks a little like Catherine Deneuve. If Catherine Deneuve was glassy-eyed from antidepressants and evening cocktails. I listen for hours. Just the buzz of condo appliances.

The only other thing I hear my father say late in the evening is, "I've got late work to attend to."

And my mother going, in a voice even I have to admit is filled beautifully with tiny nails, "Your work takes you from the house in ways you positively relish." Then the door slams. Then

I hear the sound of unscrewing. Vodka? Scotch? Courvoisier? What're we drowning in tonight, Mother? I really don't blame her. If I was stuck in some kind of psychotic housewife hell in a condo with nothing but rich people objects to clean while a philandering husbandaid escaped for his nightly escapades ... I'd medicate the shit out of myself. Or just check out. For real.

I open my bedroom door a crack to spy on her. Ah. Well, I approve. She's gone with Jim Morrison's favorite booze. Live it up, Mother. She looks ... she looks like she's melting into the chair. She looks like a Francis Bacon painting.

She wasn't always a melted face. My mother, I mean. She used to be wicked smart. Read all kinds of books. And she was a concert pianist. When they got with each other. Apparently. That's why a baby grand lives with us in the condo. But I haven't heard her play since I was five. When I was born she had some kind of breakdown. Then when I was ten she ate an entire bottle of sleeping pills. I remember watching my father slap her face trying to wake her up. I remember how she looked lying on the hardwood floor, her body in a little "s" shape. I remember going into the bathroom and eating toilet paper and crying.

After that she just sort of became an expert at rubbing things clean. That baby grand? Silent but spotless.

When I was five ... jesus christ was I ever five?

I'm five and my mom and dad have me decked out in some kind of black velvety girl-dress and black patent-leather mary jane shoes and my hair is long and blond and captured in a beautiful black satin bow. I have no idea what I look like to all the adults around us but I'm praying to the moon I look "pretty."

We are at one of my mother's solo piano performances.

My father and I sit on red velvet chairs, part of the "audience." Everyone's eyes are on my mother. Everyone's heart is on my mother. Everyone's leaning forward toward her, her face, her body, her hands, waiting to be pleasured. Her back is straight and strong. Her hair is wrapped up and around in great swirls of French twist. Her gown is off-white silk and chiffon, and off of her shoulders, so that her shoulders look to me like perfect pearl drops. Everyone is holding their breath in anticipation.

No one is everyone more than I am. I am hot underneath my black velvet and a little itchy and yep a little bit I have to pee but I'm also wanting. I could eat her. I want to run up that instant and crawl into her lap and fold my face between her jaw and collarbone and suck on her shoulder.

When her hands lift and then lower onto the keys and the first notes sound I think I might die. I start crying.

My father gently, so gently, puts his hand on my leg and whispers, "Shhhh sweetheart, it's OK, it's OK." He puts his arm around me. He's right, it is, but five-year-olds can't contain all the pleasure and pride and happiness I am feeling in their minds or bodies yet so now I'm not just crying; I'm peeing, just a little, not enough for any kind of scene or anything, but enough to relieve some of this motherloving godforsaken pressure.

She is beautiful. She is playing franz shoe burt.

She is beautiful she is beautiful sheisbeautifulbeautiful-beautifulbeautiful.

When she is finished playing franz shoe burt I can't hold anything in anymore and I leap out of my red velvet seat which has the faintest trace of girl pee on it and I squeeze through the aisle of pretty dressed-up people clapping and I run up to the stage and I crawl on up her leg, knee, into her lap and she's laughing and people are clapping and she's kissing me and holding me and a little bit I put my mouth on one of her shoulders and a little bit I'm about to suck her shoulder and then we both stand up and she holds my hand and looks down at me smiling and signals me and miraculously I know what to do.

We bow.

Together.

I PUNCH HER number into my cell. "Hello," she goes.

"Hello," I go.

"Ida," she says.

"Mother," I respond.

"Ida?" she asks.

"Yes, Mother?"

"Is there something you want to say?" she asks.

"I just … just wanted to say hello, I guess …" I stare at my ceiling.

"All right then," she says, her voice barely audible.

"Bye," I go, but she's already gone.

I stick my phone in my ass pocket. I look up again at the vag crack on my ceiling. I dig inside my backpack and pull out a spoon. Yep, you know whose spoon. I put the spoon in my mouth for lubrication.

I close my eyes.

I picture Obsidian. Her hair black as a record album falling down on my face. The stone of her necklace jabbing my throat. Then I unzip my pants and pull down my deal and spoon-rub my twinkle till it's red. I'm a fucking daughter of Eve.

Dizzy.

White.

Vibrate.

I grab my cell from my backpack, my pants around my thighs. "Obsidian?" I go. Silence. "Obsidian?"

But it's just my own ass calling me.

7.

SOME MEETINGS I LIE, SOME MEETINGS I FLIRT, AND some meetings I box. With the Sig.

Think about it. Psychotherapists – they're all hot for your deepest darkest secrets anyway, so the more you lie, the happier they are. It gives them the chance to *delve*. *Penetrate*. Use weird hand gestures. Write crap down. And the whole set-up of this doctor/patient shit is completely porno. You spill your guts and cry like a pussy while they "father you better." Christ. How is that different than Mrs. K. ass-up in my father's study? Yeah. I'm pretty sure the word for that is subjugation. Marlene taught it to me.

All I'm saying is that you've got to get the upper hand in these deals or you are screwed.

Anyway. Today Sig's hell-bent on talking about my black-outs, so the gloves are off. Turns out that's the only part of my story he's interested in. Letcho. But there's no fucking way I'm telling him anything about Obsidian. Like ever. Whatever comes out of his pie-hole, I will motherfucking one-up it.

In his cozy little liar's den.

With oriental rugs and floor-to-ceiling book walls.

Me the girl on the couch. Catholic girl skirt with silver buckles.

Him in the blond camel-back chair. Dockers and a blue button-down. Tweed sport coat. No, I'm not kidding.

Hot girl on man mind-fuck.

Let's get ready to rumble.

We back and forth it a good while with neither of us going down. I'll give the guy this – he's persistent. He sort of hammers home with the same big-words argument until it sounds true. Oddly, big words are kind of mesmerizing. Like neuropathology. Like psychosomatic. Paramnesia. If you don't have what it takes, he could really hoodoo you into thinking that you don't know who you are.

To make sure I do not get tricked I stare at the clock behind his head. Get this. It's a cuckoo clock. Only the cuckoo doesn't shoot out like it's supposed to. It cuckoos at the top and half hours, but no bird.

He goes, "There are neuropathologies created when the psyche is in an excited state." It's 4:30. The cuckoo clock does its thing. I get up and walk over to the clock. I reach up and push on the little door. It's stuck in there. I stand on a chair and shove my fingers in the slit and try to grab that little fucker.

"It's no use," Siggy says, "it's stuck."

"So why do you have this broken fucking clock?" I ask.

"Nostalgia. It's from Vienna. My mother gave it to me. But it keeps time."

I get nostalgia. I remember hearing piano music before I could talk. I remember the smell of my father's after-shave – when he'd hoist me up onto his shoulders – I remember how I could see the world from the perch of Father. I remember laughing with his head between my little girl legs.

I sit back down on the couch across from him, but I keep my eyes on the stuck cuckoo's door. Today Siggy's got ants in his pants. He's ratcheting up the lingo, I can tell, because his voice is ever so slightly higher and tighter like someone is slowly choking him.

That's why when he says, "Ida, your hysteria is the case for sexual excitement," I have to immediately drop my gaze back down from the busted cuckoo clock with its stuck bird to his head and uppercut with, "Gee, you mean to say my giz biz is what makes me a psycho? Does it make you a psycho too? You know, when your little man salutes with a *pearly drop* on his little head?"

You got to have your junk at the ready. Like I told you, he's a sly one.

Then I make a misstep though. I tell him accidentally about some pearl earrings my dad showed me that he told me he was going to give to me, then ended up giving to Mrs. K. I know because I saw her with them on when we bumped into the Ks at a restaurant. I have no idea why I tell him that. It just sort of came out when I said "pearly drop." Goddamn it.

But you can't just *say* things in the office. He leans way forward in his camel-back chair and points his little black pen at me and goes, "Jewel drops. The gift of pearl earrings your father gave to his lover instead of you. The jewel drops are a sexual symbol for that which he has given her and not you – his affections." Then jewel drops this and jewel drops that – jewel drops dripping all over the goddamn place.

Finally I snap out of it and left-jab with, "Jeez, Sig, can you even make a sentence without your own cock in it? *Jewel drops?* Are you serious? When you're walking around in the world and you see women with earrings on, is that what you are thinking? That their ear bling is dripping with … Eeeeewwwwwwww. Dude. That's so boy teen cream dream! What are you, like seventeen?"

He counters with, "Ida, your inability to admit your jealousy of your father's lover creates a crisis in consciousness." Oh. Score. That one gives me a bit of a fat lip. There is something about Mrs. K. Her ass is … unforgettable. So white. So big. Like the moon split. I sit silent for a second on the couch across from him. My father's lover. Big white split moon ass.

But no way is he gonna take this round. I give Sig the drop dead stare and part my legs just wide enough there on the couch to flash him some teen muff before I stand up and jet across the room. Panties on a need-to-wear basis only. You gotta have an ace in the hole.

He drops his pen on the floor and coughs. Coughs. A lot.

Something sticks in his throat. He stares at his thighs and rubs them briskly. Careful not to set your pants on fire.

Bring it, old man.

I pace around his office touching things, watching his progressively more anxious reactions.

"Hey Siggy," I go, "why are you so interested in my father's ho, anyway? Do you read your notes to yourself at night and jimmy the pickle? Or are you writing it all down for a bestselling novel or something?"

"Ida." He's using the chin-down gravel voice. "These discussions are not the material for some … roman à clef."

I stop dead in my tracks. This could be interesting. "What the fuck is a roman à clef?" I go, and proceed to walk around and around his desk.

He sighs like this is all annoying him. But I know better. He loves to answer my questions. "A roman à clef, literally translated, is a novel with a key. But what it means is a novel that is based on real people from the author's life. With the names changed."

"Gimme an example," I go.

"Charlotte Brontë's *Jane Eyre*. Or Charles Dickens' *David Copperfield*."

I stare at him with lockjaw, arms crossed over my chest. Unimpressed.

"Each is a novel with a kind of … secret at its center. The secret is the author's life, embedded in fiction."

I consider this. "Does *On the Road* count?"

"I beg your pardon?"

Please tell me with all these goddamned books lining the walls you know who Jack Kerouac is. "You know, Jack Kerouac?"

"Ah. Well, yes, I suppose. And to answer your earlier query, psychotherapy is not a novel."

"But you already told me you write … what are they called … case studies? What are those?"

"Clinical recitations of patient pathologies."

"Right." I click my heels together like Dorothy and close my eyes and recite, "There's no place like home" a few times. I don't know why. Just feel like it. I stop and open one eye and give him a stink-eye for a second. "So you don't take people's lives and make them into books? With different names?"

He coughs some more. He sounds a little asthmatic. I see my opening. I do random jumping jacks.

He goes, "Ida, wouldn't you like to have a seat?"

"Thanks Siggy, I'm kinda fond of the ass I have already," I say, patting my girl-butt.

He scratches something invisible on his chest.

Keep it moving. They hate that. They like you best on the couch.

I kid-skip over to the window and pull back the curtain and look down at the street. If only I had a lollipop.

"Is there something out there that interests you?" he asks.

"No," I go, looking down at the street, "but I bet you get a big fat boner when you see the tops of your patient's heads from here."

He does the church and steeple thing with his hands. "Ida, I really don't see where you are going with this," he grumbles in the I'm-the-doctor voice with his chin down.

I don't know either, but I am willing to wait for it.

I saunter over to the bookshelf and run my hand over the spines of his books.

He sits upright. His eyebrows knitting. "Is there a title there of interest to you?" he asks a little too hopefully. Talk about nerdoid.

"Yeah," I say, pulling out a bright yellow one, "wasn't this Magnus Hirschfeld dude known as 'The Einstein of Sex?' That so rocks. Didn't he do dudes?" I turn to face him, waving the book in the air between us. "Do you do dudes? Siggy?"

Eyebrows drop. Hands between legs. Heavy exhale of

irritation. More coughing. Score. Bought myself a speechless on that one.

Next I walk casually over to his desk and turn on the desk light and let him talk to my back for a bit. Blah blah blahbiddy blah repression repression repression. Blah blah consciousness-subconsciousunconscious. Broken record.

That, my friends, is how I find the blow.

While he blathers on, I drag my finger dramatically across the surface of his desk. You know, that ol' check for dirt number. Too bad I didn't wear a little maid outfit. It's just a gag. But when I look at my finger, it isn't dirt. It's white. Powder white. Very faint, but true. If you know what you are looking at. When I suck my finger, I smile the smile of a girl who knows things. Siggy. You old dirty dog.

Uh huh, I'm saying the Sigster is into booger sugar.

Well all righty then. He knows things about me, but two can play at that game. I turn slowly around, and in the middle of his gloriously wordy smarty-guy sentences, I notice something he has not. With my finger still in my mouth, I say, looking at the clock on the wall just behind his head with its stuck cuckoo, "Um, Sig? I'm afraid our time is up."

That's right. Knockout walking out the door.

8.

OCCASIONALLY AVE MARIA'S RICH-AS-FUCK MOTHER "treats us to lunch."

On the top floor of some mega-lame high-rise downtown. About once a month. I'm pretty sure that's how often Ave Maria sees her moneyspawner. But I don't care. Rich people food is fun to photograph with your iPhone and you can steal drinks off of peoples' tables when they get up to relieve themselves.

But check it: lo and behold, just on the other side of the faux indoor garden in the center of the restaurant ... like a mini Eden but without the snake ... through the shitty-ass ficus leaves, is Sig. He's with some slick-looking business joker with ferret hair, ferret eyes. Because their backs are mostly facing us, I can see him, but he can't see me, so I do exactly what any self-respecting girl patient in my predicament would do. I pretend I have to go pee while Ave Maria's mother sucks down her third pomegranate 'tini. I stealthily remove my Zoom H4n from my Dora purse and nonchalantly embed it in the river rocks at the base of the fake Eden. With a 32 Gb SD card, it can record for days. Or when the batteries give out, whichever comes first.

Nobody watches girls like me in restaurants like that. We're somebody's daughter they pay to leave home. Whatever it is Sig and the Ferret are talking about, I'm gonna get the sound.

Lunch proceeds slowly as usual ... Ave Maria chucks cold shrimps over her shoulder when her motherpuddle isn't looking ... one even hits some old bag whose earlobes look like they might fall off of her head from the weight of the pearls. Hey! Jewel drops! When the cold shrimp beans her, the gasbag looks up briefly at the ceiling fresco as if God has crapped on her. I sip on a white Russian I snagged off a table absent of humans on my way back from the pisser.

Ave Maria's mother looks like a puffer fish. She is blowing bubbles at us … talking about something at us … something about travel abroad. Ave Maria is no doubt about to be shipped off to some private school far far away from the word "family." I look over at Ave Maria. Ave Maria is bending and unbending her spoon and making her own spit bubbles with her mouth.

As often as possible, I steal peeks at the Sig scene. The slick business weasel is waving his little rodent hands around. Siggy's shoulders look slumped to me. And his hair is all birds' nesty. He puts his head in his hands. Is it bad news? Good? It's so hard to read old people. Old men all look kinda like spent balloons to me. Happy just looks the same as sad on their faces. Wrinkled and sucked.

But then a whole man-drama happens.

This other dude comes into the restaurant. I don't mind telling you, he's a head-turner. Literally. You can see him coming from all the heads turning one by one to look at him. The kind of guy who looks like he deserves his own theme music. Basically to me he looks pretty much exactly like Paul Newman in *The Hustler*. Which Marlene showed me. Dang. Hotcha. They don't make 'em like that anymore. Though it's a toss-up really … I could also go with Steve McQueen in *Bullitt*.

When this guy walks, he walks slowly, one shoulder at a time. His hands sorta … swing … not like your hands or my hands. Treasure hands. He has on a brushed silver suit coat and black pants and a crisp white shirt. No tie. All the other manfucks in the place have ties on. Not this guy. Silver hair cut close to his head. But what gives me a pinch of glee is, he walks straight into the Sig scene. He puts his treasure hand on Sig's shoulder. I pull my iPhone out to short film it.

I kick Ave Maria under the table and lean over and go, "Hey. That's him."

She looks in the direction I'm pointing my iPhone. "Him who? Your grandpa?"

"My shrink."

She turns to look. "The hot guy or the geezard?"

"Geezard."

That's when god really does crap.

Sig, bless his deflated balloon self, stands up, embraces the man in that weird guy on guy pretend hug way, stares into his eyes for a moment, sways slightly, and fucking faints.

Yep, you heard me. The Sig drops like a log to the floor.

I know. "Holy shit holy shit," I go, slugging Ave Maria in the bicep.

"Awesome," Ave Maria goes. Her lushofamother burps and looks around making fish lips in confusion.

I suddenly feel like jumping to my feet and yelling "Herr Doktor!" at the top of my lungs. Ave Maria gets a contact high from my excitement and starts her random high notes thing. I'm telling you, I almost pee my fucking pants.

The Sig ... my Sig ... is out cold.

All kinds of hell breaks loose in the swank restaurant as crowwaiters descend to clean up the scene. It's easy to retrieve my beloved H4n. I'm invisible. I can't fucking believe my luck. Whatever that ferret dude said to Sig, it was big. And whoever that silvery guy is, he made Siggy ... swoon like a goddamned little girl. Whatever my H4n has on it is gonna be really, really good. I'm smiling so big it's obscene.

You know what? Fuck the mix tape. Things have changed. What I've got is way bigger than that. That's kid stuff. What I've got on my hands is real material. I've got ... oh hell yes. I've got a roman à clef. And the key is Sig. I'm not making a sound mix for a rave. I'm making a motherfucking man movie. Of him.

As we exit the room, Ave Maria's mother swimming us to

the door and Ave Maria shooting her high notes, I turn to face
the eaters in Eden one last time, high-kick the air for effect, and
yell, "KAPOW."

9.

IN MARLENE'S KITCHEN I TAKE THE ZOOM H4N OUT OF
my Dora purse and stand there sort of bouncing from foot to
foot like a kid. I'm excited. You know, excited like kids are when
they wake up and see snow. The H4n – it's black and sleek. It's
got a shock-resistant rubberized body. About the size of
a spy rat. If rats were spy cyborgs. There's a bitchin' LCD display
and the two mics are on the top – one points left and the other
right – towards each other – two little silver cocks.

Marlene's got an indigo silk kimono on and a blond braid
helmet – like Heidi. I mean, if Heidi was a black tranny. Marlene
showed me the Shirley Temple *Heidi*. It's awesome. Orphan
Heidi is left at her grandfather's mountain cabin by her mean
aunt, Dete. The old man is a grump. Slowly, he grows to love
Heidi. Evil Dete returns and farms Heidi out as a companion for
Klara, a rad wheelchair girl. The housekeeper, Frau Rottenmeier – yeah, I know – fucking hates Heidi. When Heidi teaches
Klara to walk again, Frau Rottenmeier tries to sell Heidi to
gypsies. But her grandfather sacks up, sells all his shit, and
finds her.

Heidi should have gone with the gypsies.

I don't have braids. Or hair. I'm still bald … more than a
chemo head though. I rub my head for luck. "You ready to hear
it?" I go, holding my finger over the playback button.

"Yes, Lamskotelet," Marlene goes, but then she says,

"Wait!" and she runs around the kitchen gathering two fluted glasses and some red shit in a bottle from the fridge.

"Um, what's that?" I say, pointing to the cough syrup-looking stuff.

"Kirsch! We are celebrating your capture!"

Kirsch, it turns out, is German for cherry water. Distilled from black morello cherries and their pits. You'd think it would taste sweet, but it doesn't. It tastes like almonds and pepper. We toast. She pours again. We toast again. She pours again. My head's kinda hot and my cheeks flush. She laughs the Marlene laugh. I laugh a laugh I've never heard come out of me before.

Whoever we are right then, I suddenly wish it wouldn't end. I grin so big I feel air all through my teeth. I push playback. The first voice is the ferret guy's from the restaurant.

The H4n goes, "What are you drinking, you wily bastard? Scotch? Lemme get you a scotch. Sigmund, I gotta tell you, you're gonna want a stiffie when you hear what I've got. It's hot, baby, I'm telling you it's hot."

"Am I to infer that the publisher has purchased my collection of case studies?"

Sound of an old man's hands rubbing briskly together.

I hit pause. I'm nervous. Who knows why? I take a deep breath. I look across the kitchen table at Marlene. She smiles. I finish off my cough syrup. I can feel it sticky on my upper lip. I hit play again.

"Think bigger, Sigmund."

Sound of ice spinning maniacally in a glass.

"I told you, I've found the ultimate case study. This is the one that will prove to be the pièce de résistance – this exquisite plum," the recorder says.

I jam my finger on the pause button of the H4n. It scoots across the table. "Plum? Which one of us is his plum?"

I sit staring at the H4n on Marlene's table. Marlene wears an expression of concern. I stand up. I sit down. "Gimme another shot of that cherry shit. I think I'm going to need it." She pours. Rain beats on the kitchen window. My head itches. My cheeks suddenly feel like fucking burning plums.

I hit playback. Siggy's voice sounds tight and screechy.

"What 'bigger picture?' Is it the publisher? Jackasses. The prestige I have brought to them over the years!"

Sound of old man fist hitting table.

"Sigmund. Sig. My friend. Settle down, will ya? It's not even about the book anymore. Books are dead, Sig, books are dead."

Sound of dishes being cleared at nearby table.

"Do you mean MY book? Is MY book dead? Listen you little money-grubbing weasel—"

Sound of tableware rattling.

I hit pause. This time I'm laughing. But my laugh sounds tight and raw.

Marlene tilts her head. "Liebchen," she asks.

"Yeah?" I go.

"Are you sure this is what you want?"

I cough. "I'm sure," I go. Something in my head ticks. Then I punch the playback.

The H4n jumps to life. "Sig! Calm down, calm down! Here – here's your drink. Drink it. No, really. Get a good gulp down. Stop waving your arms around! You don't want to make a scene, do you? Cheers, old man. Raise a glass. It's a celebration."

Sound of gulping.

"OK. You OK now? OK. Here's the gig, baby. We've been picked up. Biggest production company in television."

Sound of waiters bringing food.

"What? What in the world does that mean? What does tele-vision have to do with me?"

"What's television got to do with you? Hello? Dr. Phil? Dr. Ruth? Dr. Oz? Intervention? Television is the new paid reality, my friend. And I just bought you your ticket in. Once Oprah gets her ass out there's going to be a huge vacuum … and we're gonna fill that air, baby."

Sound of strained breathing and coughing.

Sound of hand slapping back.　　•

"Sigmund? Sig? You all right buddy? I know! I can't believe it either. You gonna make it? Sig. Buddy. Here – for christ's sake – have a little blow. It will calm you the fuck down."

Old man snorting sound. Old man coughing sound.

"Sigmund! My man! Drink some water. Lemme lay it out for you. I pitched you! Get it? They want you, Sig. They really, really, want you. One year contract in the bag. Second year optioned."

"But my book … my life's work … I would never agree to this! It's the epitome of unethical!"

"Whoa! Sig! This blows your book out of the water! Are you even listening to me? Hello? Those case studies you are so proud of? They're not going to die some dusty old death. They're going live. We're getting 'em scripted and re-enacted. One a week. We need a new 'you,' but I got that covered … and we'll need to … you know, change some stuff around so we don't get our asses sued or anything, but …"

"It's unethical. It's out of the question."

Sound of old man slamming scotch.

"What did you mean by a 'new me'?"

"It's big money."

Coughing.

"Big. Money."

Coughing.

"The clincher is your teen little-monster girl. The other case studies look like zombies compared to her. So the only catch is, you have to bag that one. I mean nail that girl. When I told them what she looks like and the kind of shit she pulls? POW. Without her, we don't have shit."

I'm across the kitchen by now. "STOP it," I yell. Marlene jams her blue-lacquered nail on the pause button. The H4n slides across the table like it's trying to run. I stomp back to the table. I pick the H4n up. I want to punch it or throw it across the room. I slam it back down. I begin to cough. Hack, actually.

Whoppers. "Rewind it." Marlene rewinds. "Play that shit again. Because I can't believe my fucking ears."

Before I realize what I'm doing I pick up the bottle of cough syrup and chuck it across the room. It shatters like kid wishes all over her white wall.

"Lamskotelet!" Marlene says.

I stare at the red stain I've made. Fucking Rorschach.

"Fuck. I'm sorry." I get all down on the floor and start picking up the glass shards. My throat gets tight. My head feels like it has a rubber band around it. My eyes are watering like a girl's. I'm coughing and coughing. I cut my hand pretty much immediately. Of course. Marlene comes over and takes my hands in hers and walks me to the kitchen sink. She runs cold water over my hand and thumb. Blood rivers down her drain.

"Everybody uses everybody until we're all just a bunch of used up shit sacks waiting to go to dirt," I go.

Marlene doesn't say anything. She dries my hands. She reaches under the sink and gets a first aid kit and wraps my cut-up hand with a gauze bandage, slowly. I stare at the little red cleft in my hand. *Don't cry, pussy*.

Then a numb comes. It's a numb I know. It's the numb of a girl checking out. Whatever they say next can't fucking touch me. I'm long gone. One way or another, I will end this. But on my terms. I turn the volume up. Marlene picks up glass on the floor. The next voice is Sig's. His voice is all over the map.

"I find that last comment entirely offensive. This is intolerable. You have no right to talk about any client in such a way—"

For a second I think the Sig is going to rescue me. Like Heidi's Grandpa. Can you beat that?

"—but what was it you said earlier – what did you mean a new 'you?' You mean me?"

"New you? What I meant was, well we can't … Sig, I mean, look. You're one big brain with a whole fucking library of shit stuck up in that noggin, but you're not exactly a visual magnet, right? But don't worry about that. I found someone – another client of mine – who is *very* interested. He was *made* for TV. Oh – and he's in your line of work."

"You found an actor who is a psychotherapist?"

"What? Fuck no. I found a dream guy. What's that shit you ordered? Is that the Chicken Kiev? It looks like paste. All this frou-frou new food looks like crap to me. I should have ordered a fucking steak."

Sound of old man half choking on food.

"Symbols and brain waves and talkity talk. Like you. Only he's a looker. No offense. Actually, you already know each other. Hey! Look! Here he comes now. Hope you don't mind, I invited him to join us. To share the news … I'll get us all another round."

Sound of chairs being pushed back.

I steal a glance at Marlene. I remember from the restaurant. It's the silvery hot guy. I crank the volume.

"Sigisimund! My old friend. So very good to see you!"

"My … I … Jung?"

Sound of body falling to the floor.

The H4n shuts off.

Marlene looks at me.

I look at Marlene.

"That's where he fucking fainted," I go.

"Liebchen, are you well?" she asks.

I bend down on the ground. I calmly put my beloved H4n – maybe the only thing in the world besides Marlene that I trust – into my backpack. I stand up. I look out of the kitchen window. I wish it was snowing. I mean I wish it kid hard. But it's still just stupid raining. Well, there's more than one place to find white stuff.

Marlene and I lock eyes.

"Marlene?" I go.

"Liebchen?" she answers.

"I'm gonna need to borrow one of your wigs. Can you help me pick one? One that, you know, will make me not look anything like me?"

"Certainly. I happen to be very good at disguises. Who do you want to look like?" she asks.

I suck some blood on my thumb. Almond pepper. Kirsch Wasser.

"Dora," I go. "I want to look like Dora. They want a show, I'll give them one."

IO.

IF YOU WANT TO STALK SOMEONE PROPER, ONE WORD
for you: wigs.

Lucky for me, Marlene's got lots of 'em. She's got platinum
blond Marilyn Monroes and fire-engine red beehives and long
jet blacks with Bettie Page bangs. She's got blue hair and pink
hair and hair the color of purple Slurpees. She's got a foot wide
'fro and a spiky punk black and blue. She's got Liz Taylors and
Zsa Zsas. She's got long hair and short hair and tall hair and soft
trusses and bobs and shags and even this braid down to your ass
that would make a man yell RAPUNZEL half a mile away.

Obviously she uses them for her gigs at the tranny jazz club.
I have other plans. With a wig, you can be anyone.

My mother once lost all of her hair. It came out in patches
at first, then great clumps. So she cut it short–then it began
to look refugee. They said it was psychosomatic. They said it was
stress. They said she made her own hair fall out of her head.
It happened three years ago. When my father made his choice
with Mrs. K.

It grew back the next year. Slowly. But her eyes never were
the same.

There's a book my mother read to me as a kid. At least at
first. I still have it. It's under my bed. It's a little trashed, but still
cool. *Are You My Mother?* You know it? It's about a pathetic baby
bird. The kid bird hatches while the mom is gone out of the nest.
He's clueless. He goes looking for her. He asks a kitten, a hen, a

dog, and a cow if they are his mother. They go, "No." Then he asks a shitty old car, a boat and a plane, and at last, a fucking power shovel. The shovel dumps him back into his nest and the absent mother returns.

It's a good book. But the kid bird is pretty much an idiot.

Marlene's got an-old school man's silk smoking jacket on and a Marlene Dietrich wig and a cigarette in a long thin cig holder.

Three magnificent wigs sit on her kitchen table, staring up at us, headless.

I look down at the wigs on Marlene's table. I rub my stubbled head. This is the closest I have ever come to looking like my mother. Er, how she did hairless, anyway. Sometimes I think that's why I did it. Whatever. I study the wig selections.

Wig one: a black-as-crows chin-length blunt cut. Very smarty-looking. Would look great with black-rimmed smarty glasses and a shiny black raincoat. And boots. Kinda Emma Peel from *The Avengers*.

Wig two: shoulder-length strawberry with color weave highlights – kinda preppy. Would need a cashmere sweater and a thin strand of pearls. Think Molly Ringwald in *The Breakfast Club*.

But it's wig three that's dominating the others. Totally badass feathered and frosted. Christ. It's so … man. It's so hot … it's so 80s … it's so motherfucking Ultimate Farrah. It looks like it might lift off the table, achieve loft, and fly around the room.

"Think I could pull that bad boy off?" I say, pointing to it. "What do they even call that, frosted?" The other wigs look dejected and jealous.

"That depends," Marlene says, tilting her head to the side, touching her blue Lee nails against her Coca-Cola red lips, "if you wear this you will turn heads. People can't help themselves. They are nostalgic for the times with big hair."

"Yeah, I know what you mean … that's not necessarily a good thing …"

"When trying not to be seen." She taps her lips. Her eye-lashes seem longer than my thumbs.

"Yup."

"On the other hand," Marlene walks around the table of wigs, inspecting them, kinda picking at the other two, "it looks the least like you, Lamskotelet. Your Herr Doktor would never recognize the you under this hair. No one would. Not even I would." She strokes the wings of it.

We stare at it there on the table.

I lift the Farrah up off of the table, balancing it on my fist, and hold it slightly higher than my skull in front of me. It shimmers under the kitchen light. Its wings positively radiant. It asks me its question. Can you be me?

Somehow it is very solemn, this choice, who to be, who not to be.

"Come, we will try it," Marlene says, and shoulders me toward the bathroom mirror.

The second it's on my head we both know it. I don't care if I have to wear a fucking jumpsuit with platforms and sing Bee Gees. Sometimes you just know things. This is the one.

First of all, it's heavy. In a good way. Like you are more important than usual. And my whole face looks different. I look like a woman with feathered bangs. A woman who will wear a lot of mascara and eyeliner. A woman who is going to need a shitload of lip gloss. But there's something else going on, too.

I stare at this self in the mirror, Marlene just behind me. You know, in life? Whoever you're gonna be, I think maybe the trick is to be it over the top. Maybe that's part of my problem. I'm me, but I'm me like 50 per cent. I'm out there, but I fade. I cough. I look away. I pass out.

Little Teena, he's on HIGH VOLUME no matter where he goes or what he does. Ave Maria is doped to the nines most of the time so I have no idea who she is, but at least she's unforget-table. You can hear her high notes in your ears long after she's gone. Marlene, well, Marlene can be a man and then turn woman like day turns to night. Shabazz. Obsidian is so Obsidian it feels like she could kill you if you even breathed like you didn't care. Black hair. Black eyes. Black shard of fuck you dangling from her neck.

Me? I'm Ida. Angry messed up Ida with the dumb-sounding voice. I'm Dora the Explorer. I'm the girl who has to go to therapy. The most me thing about me is my technological ... gear. Who the fuck am I even?

Almost like she's in my head with me, Marlene goes, "This," standing behind me in the mirror reflection with her hands in my new hair, "is the you that will make a film. Daughter of Eve!"

I don't know why but standing there like that under the breath of her sentence makes me feel like I'm real. I wonder if that's what love is.

Marlene takes in a great breath of air and claps her hands above our heads and says, "Bacon! To celebrate!"

When I wheel around to follow, I can feel the hair swing. Like it's part of me. Big. Heavy. WINGS.

Back in the kitchen, Marlene scoops up the wig heads off of the table and throws them onto a nearby chair. They look like roadkill.

Whoever we are right then, I suddenly wish it wouldn't end.

I grin so big I feel air all through my teeth. I shake the hair back. In my head there's a lame-ass little bird, chirping its fucking head off, happy.

II.

IN THE HALLWAY IN FRONT OF THE SIG'S OFFICE I STUDY
the wood of his door. It looks like skin. I put my hand on it without making a sound. On the other side of the door, is he waiting?
I make my hand into a fist and pound the fuck out of the door.

Frankly, when he opens it? He looks agitated. And what is
up with that hair? New wave bird's nest.

"Siggy!" I yelp, blowing by him into the office. I have a present for him under my arm – all wrapped up like for birthdays.
I jam it into his chest. Oh for christ's sake. I think he's blushing.
"Oh Sig," I say, "don't go getting all soft on me. It's not anything
weird. G'head, open it."

He struggles with the paper exactly like the old man bofus
he is. This gives me exactly enough time to loiter over by his
trench coat hanging by the door. I slip my hand into my Dora purse
and then slip a GoTEK7 GPS into the pocket of his flasher coat.

The GoTEK7 is a very small, personal and powerful live
tracking GPS device allowing you to track assets, vehicles or people. It is lightweight and water-resistant. It is also fitted with a
discreet panic alarm; once pressed for four seconds the device
will inform you of its location via your mobile phone or a PC, giving you peace of mind with loved ones.

I scan the room. Half-smoked stogie in the ashtray on his
desk. Busted fucking cuckoo clock doing its nothing.

He finally has the wrapping off.

"It's a clock," he says.

Braniac.

"Yep. Cuz of your busted cuckoo." I grab the clock out of his hands and take it to the big man desk and position it. "You like?"

Really, it's not handsome. It's this weird painted crap gold color and kind of the shape of a boil. I mean it sorta rises up in the middle and slopes down on the sides with these bizzaro ornate carvings of lions. I got it at a vintage shop … who knows if the fucker will even work beyond today. Inside is a covert camera with built-in video recorder that can use any USB storage device – an iPod, a Sony PlayStation, memory cards, PCs, external hard drives, you name it. You'd be amazed how all the tricky old school Cold War spy crap has been transformed into modern-day techno gadgetry available online for $49.99.

Sig makes some incredibly awkward attempt to thank me from across the room. I make my way over toward the credenza with all the tea-making crap on it. A tea pot. Mugs. A variety of bullshit bouge teabags. Sugar. Milk. A spoon. Pretty much everything I need.

"Lemme make it this time," I offer. "What'll it be?" I finger his teabags.

With my back to him, I pull a vial of booger sugar out from my Dora reticule. "Earl Grey? Jasmine? Lemon ginger? Passionfruit? What say we go with passionfruit. Get a little wild. Sugar?" I go, looking back at him over my shoulder. He nods appreciatively. God, old man balls are easy to snow. It's actually quite sad.

Next I pull out the Viagra of Hakizamana Ojo. Marlene's pills. "I got a bitchin' dream to lay on you, Sig," I say, crushing the pills – one, two, three of 'em – with the back of a spoon, carefully re-collecting it, and putting it into his tea. I go slowly and I take extra care. I rim the mugs with the spoon. The porcelain circle sound is something between mesmerizing and shoot yourself. I tap the cup with the spoon. This soundscape is going to be *awesome*.

"SO," I go, "Lemme tell you about my dream." I walk over

to him, bend over, and serve him tea. "Trust me Siggy. You are going to LOVE this shit."

He sips. He smiles the smile of a man who is being served.

I smile and cock my head, try to look like the niece he blathers on about so much. Gag me. "You ready for the dream junk?"

"Proceed." Look at that smug fuck. You want it? You got it.

"So check it out. A house was on fire. My father was standing beside my bed and woke me up. I dressed myself quickly. Mother wanted to stop and save her jewel case, but Father said: 'I refuse to let myself and my child be burnt for the sake of your jewel case.' We hurried downstairs, and as soon as I was outside I woke up." I sit bolt upright and stare at him with the biggest eyes I can muster. "Isn't it cool as shit?"

He thinks it's remarkable. He rubs his hands together. He's way into it. God. I can see him revving up his interpretation jazzy jizz. And yep, just like I think he will, he goes straight for the jewel case. And just like I knew he would, he says it's a vag. I can't help it. I start laughing. But when I look over at him, he's all serious and shit. He thinks laughter is a defensive mechanism. "Sorry," I say. And bite the inside of my cheek.

"Ida, what is it about the jewel case that your mother wanted to save?" He continues all Dr. Big-head-y.

I go, "My dad gave it to her. She has buttloads of bling, trust me. Which is mega stupid, since they rarely go out or do anything together. I think he piles up the bling to ease his guilt about balling Mrs. K. It just sits there piling up in the case getting dusty. Sometimes she pets the pile, though."

His cheeks flush. He drinks his tea. His pupils – dang, I think his pupils are dilating! He says, "And do you find any other associations with a jewel case?"

I look up at the ceiling. "Hey, you know you have a crack in your ceiling that looks like a big huge wang?" I point.

"Might you answer the question?"

"Might you?" I go, smiling. Then I give him more of what

59

he wants. "Yeah. Mr. Fucking Fuckface K. gave me a jewelry box once. A really gross expensive one. From Vienna. I put weed in it. Hey! Want some more tea?"

I jump up. I run over like a dutiful niece. I refill his cup. I take my time. I can feel his eyes on my back when he theorizes that a return present was subconsciously due to Mr. K. No shit, Sherlock.

"Really." I go, stirring, stirring.

"Perhaps you do not know that 'jewel case' is a favorite expression for the same thing that you wear daily – the ... reticule."

I turn to deliver more tea to him. "What the fuck's a reticule?"

He laughs all sly and adult. He says, "In chiefly historical terms, a reticule is a woman's small handbag. In other words, the jewel case and the reticule are both symbols of female genitalia."

I roll my eyes and snort-laugh. "Siggy! Dude! You *always* say shit like that! So you are saying Mr. K. gave me a pussy box for pussy? And it showed up all weird in my dream? And my Dora bag is a VAG, too?"

Mind-bogglingly, he grins and keeps going. "In the dream you chose a situation which expresses a danger from which your father is saving you."

Holy shit. He thinks he's ... what do old guys like him think? He looks like he thinks he's solved a really, really hard cross-word puzzle. Dude. Are you for real? Is in my head. But "Wow ..." is all I say.

To this he leans in real stern-like and flourishes with, "The dream confirms once more that you are summoning up your old love for your father in order to protect yourself against your repressed love for Mr. K."

I stare at him.

He drinks his tea.

I consider applauding. Or just barfing. I'm pretty good at barfing on command.

Instead, I lean in toward him. "Sig," I say all serioso, "Do people really buy this crap you feed them? That purses and jewelry boxes are *vagz*?" I ask him.

Uh oh. Soft crotch alert for the Sig. He flicks invisible lint off of his shoulder. "I didn't say the actual objects are genitals. I said they represent them in the subconscious. In dreams."

Come to mamma. I have him now. I stand up. I walk around the room in a circle. I can feel his stare. On my boots. On my calves. My ass covered only with teen plaid punk skirt. Then I walk across the room near his desk. I turn toward him. I put my hand on my Dora the Explorer purse hanging at my twat and pat it hard. "Reticule ..." I murmur. "I see." I smile. Then I pick up what is left of his manky-ass cigar in his little ashtray and suck it. "Sssssshhhhhhhhttttttt-O-gie," I go, and pantomime a Groucho Marx. "What's that make your cigar, Herr Doktor?"

He stands up. He sits down and flaps his hands around in the air. "Ida, we are not in the process of discussing random objects in a room ..." he babbles, but I cut him off. I'm moving in for the kill. Watch it. I'm not your niece, old man. I'm your worst teen nightmare. And I know a thing or two about the art of interpretation.

"No? Why not? I'd wager a fatty that the objects in this room – the porn cracks in the ceiling, the half-smoked stub of a cigar – I mean who smokes cigars anymore – just crusty old farts, Siggy, are you a crusty old fart? C'mon! You and what's in your pants are very much part of this discussion. You old dog, you. You really want to talk about reticules and jewel cases with young girls. I bet talking about it gets you all hot. I bet you own the complete works of Aubrey Beardsley. Wanna know what I think of your theory here, Sig? I think it's all about dick."

Then a sound cracks the air between us. Cough. Über loud cough from Sig. "Ida," he tries, but his cough cuts him off. Cough. Coughing. Coughity cough can't stop.

I rush over. I slap his back a high hard one. "You OK, Sig?" I slam-pat his back. His face reddens. He bends over with coughing. "More tea!" I go and shuttle him over another cup. He gulps and gulps. After a sputtering coupla minutes, he manages to breathe and collect himself.

Me? I'm sitting calmly on the black leather couch like the most polite and normal girl on the entire fucking planet. Legs crossed, hands folded over knees. Churchlike.

As if on cue, the spy clock chimes. It sounds something like birds shitting tin.

"Well," I offer, "that was quite an interpretation. You really do have the synaptic wizardry, Herr Doktor, that's for damn sure." I put my chin on top of my fist. "I'll have to go think about all that. No, don't get up ... I can let myself out. You have a seat. Man alive. You sure got the big head."

I rise.

I turn.

My parting words: "Keep it up, Doc. That's what you're good at."

12.

WHEN I EXIT SIG'S, I WALK EXACTLY ONE BLOCK TO
where Ave Maria's mom's Jag is parked and waiting for me. I can
see Little Teena in the driver's seat as I approach. I can see
Ave Maria in the back seat. And I can see both of the wigs they are
wearing.

Uh huh, it occurs to me what I'm doing is over the line. Uh
huh, I think about the possible consequences of my actions. For
a moment I fear for the Sigster. What would a lethal overdose of
Viagra look like? I earlier read on the Internet some dangerous
side effects ... he could pass out. Go into a coma. He could go
blind. A few guys have actually died. My throat gets a little tight
and my chest feels like someone is pushing on it. I think about
Sig going coronary.

But you know what I think about more? I think about all
the times in my life I didn't understand what the fuck was happening and no one bothered to explain it to me. Like when I got
my period. I thought I was dying of cancer. My gym teacher
took me into his office and explained it to me. Yeah. That's what
you want. You want some balding old creep explaining your
bleeding vag back to you while some middle school lunch lady
comes in shoving a giant cotton pad in your face and telling you
to put it between your legs, dear. Awesome.

I think about Mr. K. trying to stick his Altoid tongue down
my throat on a lakeside picnic – no one rescuing me from the
lakeside letch. I mean I had to pop that guy right in the nose hard

enough to make his eyes water. I was fourteen. There are no superheroes.

I keep walking toward the car and the posse. Family is a word you can make your own.

I can hear the purr of the Jag's engine.

I think about all the shit that goes wrong in the world today that teens have to endure.

Like how Ave Maria's stepdad used to give her a bath – wash her real good – when she was like four. Five. Six. And film it. Home movies.

How when Little Teena told his über Christian parents he was gay all the way, they told him the devil had him and sent him to some weird military school compound. Then they went away for the summer on a wine tour in Germany and spread some word of god seed. While Little Teena took three bottles of pharmaceuticals and had his stomach pumped. Enjoy that case of Gewürztraminer, Mr. and Mrs. Jesus Fuck?

Remember the Josef Fritzl case? The Austrian daddy who made a prison in his basement for his daughter? Yeah. He fathered her good. Seven children and one miscarriage. I keep wondering. What's it like to be a forty-two-year-old woman who comes out of the basement and tells that story? And who were the bastard fucks living next door who *didn't … see … a … thing*?

Boohoo, right? Life's not fair. Well life's not supposed to be a fucking Disney-gone-bad horror ride where you are trapped in a car called "family" with creepola psycho adults popping out at you at every turn either now, is it? Look at the world ride you've made for your children. No wonder we want your drugs. It's the least you can do.

So yeah, I think about what I'm doing. What I'm doing is opening the door of Ave Maria's mom's Jag and getting in. It's like I told you. We stage art attacks. It's not like we're terrorists. At least not the way you think.

I climb into the Jag. My Farrah wig and clothes are on the back seat, waiting for me.

"We locked and loaded?" Little Teena asks from the driver's seat.

"Ready!" Ave Maria pitches a high note at me. There's a compact suitcase on the seat between us. She pats the top of it.

I look at my comrades for a long minute. God. I love them so.

Ave Maria wears the Molly Ringwald wig from Marlene's, offset with wire-rimmed glasses.

Up front is what can only be described as the head of Julia Child. It's some weird, tall, big-curled tower of a wig that makes Little Teena look like somebody's grandmother. Somebody's very scary man-in-drag grandmother. He's driving one-handed, arm extended. Somehow he's fit his girth into a sharp navy-blue women's business suit. Complete with hose and pumps. Oh, and he's got a false police detective badge. Nice touch.

"Oh yeah," I go, "we're locked and loaded." And begin my transformation.

Inside the Jag I strip. Little Teena hums the striptease song from the driver's seat. The windows immediately fog up. I stretch my legs down and my hips up until I can see my own underwear – leopard print. I pull on a pair of white denims. Bell bottoms. Which to be honest, I didn't think still existed. Then I dive into a pink angora sweater and shoot my head out, a little fuzz in my mouth. I strap on a pair of Candy wedgie sandals. Then I don the sacred Farrah wig. Head down, wig on, flip up.

Ave Maria opens up the little suitcase between us, rummages around, then hands me a pair of owl-eyed brown sunglasses and some cherry lip gloss. I put the sunglasses on and butter up my smacker.

Next she hands me my Bluetooth. We've all got matching Bluetooths like little ear tumors. Communication is essential when you're on a mobile shoot.

I look at myself in the rear view from the backseat. If I was anymore 1970s I'd be whoever my mother was.

Obsidian's not in the car. She's on the way. Obsidian's talking to us through our Bluetooths. Sometimes her voice in my ear makes my breath jack-knife. When she says the word "Ida," I get dizzy.

In the Jag, with a laptop in the back seat, parked and holding, we track the Sig.

Because of the clock with the hidden micro cam I put on his office desk.

Because of the GPS I put in his trenchcoat.

Because of ... spiked tea.

"Pull him up on the screen," I go.

Ave Maria and I lean in to study the computer screen like doctors.

Ave Maria gasps. What we see: a tiny cartoon old man frantically pacing around his office with a boner so big he looks like he's grown a third fucking leg.

He creeps over to his desk and tries to sit down. No luck getting that bad boy to behave. He limps his way over to the camel-backed chair and braces himself. He looks down at it. "Um, is he crying?"Ave Maria says, and then starts laughing. "Holy fuck," she says, "He can barely walk!" Little Teena produces a stoner laugh.

I watch my Sig waddle over to the black leather Italian couch. He kinda half kneels like his back is out, then lurches, then drops and rolls himself in an attempt to lie down. "Christ," I shout, "it's a whopper! Look at that goddamn thing!" We laugh like teens.

On the couch is an alien. A mutant. A man whose very pants are overtaking him. He tosses and turns with his arm over his face. He grabs at it. "Whoa," I yell, "he's gonna try to steer it!" I twirl my Farrah hair around my finger violently. I silently wonder if he's going to cum in his own face like Old Faithful.

"Lemme see that shit," Little Teena says from up front. I position the laptop on the seat so he can see it.

"Holy mother of god!" Little Teena bellows. "He's on the floor! On all fours! He's ... he's trying to make it to the door? Wait! He's grabbed the trenchcoat ... wait for it, wait for it, he's

UPRIGHT, folks," Little Teena announces boxing-match style. We laugh our asses off.

"Turn the engine on and pull up," I go. "Switch to the GPS tracker." Ave Maria mans the laptop in the back seat, and shazzam. Sig becomes a pulsing red throb on a virtual city on the computer screen.

Now here is where you separate the boys from the men. For this mobile shoot to work, we've got to have stamina. We've got to wait for it. I figure minimum an hour, maximum, two. Yeah, I know all the ads say "if your erection lasts longer than four hours," but Sig's a Dr. So I'm guessing he's too anal to wait four hours sitting alone in his office with a monster dong.

We shoot the shit in the car. Ave Maria's mom's having migraines. Meaning our stock of headbanger reduction pills just got filled. Little Teena's almost saved up enough for the Nikon D3X Digital SLR camera. The Expeed image processing on that bad boy assures breathtakingly rich image fidelity and reduces noise, even at high ISOs. I narrate a little of what I've read from Marlene's Mantegazza book. "Check it. Mantegazza used to prescribe coca to his patients. He wrote that to a man in imminent danger of losing his life through nervous exhaustion, he'd dope him up to the nines. Said coca was like a billion times superior to opium."

"Whoa," Ave Maria goes.

Just under two hours later, we have movement.

Ave Maria puts her finger on the red pulsing dot. It jumps around frenetically. "I wish he'd make up his mind," Ave Maria complains, "he's in, he's out, then in again … what's he doing in there? Gyawd. Is he OCD?"

I rub a see hole in my window with my angora elbow.

From the front Little Teena laughs and rips a mega fart.

Ave Maria wails. "You douche! Ooooooohhhhhhhh maaaa-aaaaan, dude! You fucking hotboxing us? Open the fucking windows!"

When my window lowers I see my doctor's front building door open a crack. "Shut up! It's him!" I go.

"What the fuck?" Little Teena says.

Nothing comes out of the door.

Nothing.

Nothing.

But we all know there's a man behind that crack.

I'm holding my breath, then realize it, then curse myself, then do it again.

"Fuck," I say, "it's the cheese …" Because a cop car pulls up. But it's not a cop car. It's a black and white taxi cab. That's when I see my shrink, my nemesis, my Sig exit the building. I get a baffling chest pang and my heart races like I'm on fucking speedies.

But what comes out of the building I'm not ready for. What comes out of the building looks something like a medieval figure. Like a creature that might ascend a tower and you know, ring the bells. A perfect Quasimodo.

"Holy jesus fuck," whispers Little Teena.

There in front of us, wearing a truly flasher trench coat, is the Sig, trying old-man desperately to shove his dick down one leg of his pants. Trying to drape the bottom of the trenchcoat over his bulging crotch. Pushing the brown trenchcoat fabric down while it pushes back up with Hitleresque authority.

"He looks crippled," Ave Maria whispers. We crack up again, but we also get low in the car and try to keep our laughing quieter.

Sig looks one way, then the other, then sort of launches himself into the cab, losing a shoe, the cab ripping away with a screech.

"Holy holy fuck," repeats Little Teena. "Are you fucking getting this? You recording?"

"Oh shit," I yell, realizing I'm sitting in the car like a dumb blond NOT FILMING OR RECORDING DICK.

That's when god appears. If god were an outrageously gorgeous angry Native American girl with a sheath of ebony hair and a shard of black slit-your-throat glass around her neck.

Obsidian yanks my door open and blasts her way into the car and shoves me over going, "GO GO GO! I got it! I got it all!" with a hand-held mini digi-cam cupped beautifully in her hand. We're all grabbing our ears since she's both shouting at us via Bluetooth and shouting at us for realz.

"Floor it!" I go. My ears and skin ringing with longing for a girl with ink-black hair who would never, ever wear a wig.

Under the maze of Seattle's snaking overpasses we plunge. Past the baseball field with the giant metal fish architecture. Through the dumb-ass tunnels wearing dangling ivy. Rain making everything blurry.

"I got ten bucks that says he's going to the Blue Ball up on Capitol Hill," Little Teena wagers.

"The SM club? No way. I say he's going up to the bouge gay hook-up park – to buy a buttload of downers. Or get that monster sucked off. Besides, ten bucks is a pussy bet. Make it fifty and you're on," Obsidian says. My mouth fills with spit and admiration.

"Yep, it's the Blue Ball," Little Teena says from the front as we run a red light in pursuit. "And I'll take that bet."

"You're full of shit. Look. We're headed straight for the park," Obsidian counters.

"Hot Tamales, anyone?" Ave Maria produces a box and doses us with cinnamon.

I study the computer screen. We're not going to the Blue Ball. Or the hook-up park. We're on Seneca Street. We're in traffic. We're gonna be fucked for a parking place. We're going to Virginia Mason Clinic – downtown Seattle. ER. I know. How? That's where they took my mom when she ate her bottle of pills. "It's a hospital target," I say.

In the car I riffle off instructions: "We're gonna have to stage a recon by triangulating. We'll be in the ER, remember, so you gotta go with the mise-en-scène. You gotta post your-selves … you gotta go both guerilla and cinéma vérité.

Obsidian? You get the micro cam. Little Teena? You pin one to your shoulder like cops do. I got the H4n and ... Ave Maria, you got the spy cam?"

She nods and spits a wad of Hot Tamales out the window of the Jag. Then she snags a costume from the small suitcase. "A hospital! I'm perfect, I'm perfect!" she shouts.

I have to admit it, her outfit kicks ass. She holds up a weird striped pinafore of some sort. At least I think that's what it is. "Where'd you fucking get that ... that apron thing?" I ask. "It's awesome."

She flips her shoulder-length strawberry-blond hair and begins to change into her costume. "It's a candy-striper suit. Get it? I like the way it makes me look Florence Nightingale-y."

I laugh. She doesn't look Florence Nightingale-y. She kinda looks like she shoulda been in *Friday the 13th, Part I*.

Little Teena rubs his false detective's badge and speeds up. "*Serpico*," he goes.

I shake my hair back like a perfect Breck girl. Obsidian captures her black mane with a scrunchie.

We all know exactly who we are.

Except then in the back of the Jag Obsidian rubs my thigh, making friction. My breathing gets weird. All up in my throat instead of my chest. Fuck. Please god of girls please do not let me pass out. I take a huge-ass breath in. I put my head down. The Farrah hair is so heavy it feels like I might suffocate.

I put one hand on each white denim thigh. Palms up. I rub my cherry lip gloss lips together. I close my eyes. I breathe in for seven seconds. I hold my breath for seven seconds. I breathe out for seven seconds. I breathe in for seven seconds. Hold it. I do it seven times. I think maybe my mother taught me this when I was seven but can't be sure.

There's a girl calm people don't know about. It's a girl teen standstill. A motionless peace. It doesn't come from anywhere but inside us, and it only lasts for a few years. It's born from being not a woman yet. It's free flowing and invisible. It's the eye of the violent storm you call *my teenage daughter*. In this place we are undisturbed by all the moronic things you think about us. Our voices like rain falling. We are serene. Smooth. With more perfect hair and skin than you will ever again know. Daughters of Eve.

When I open my eyes, I'm girl clear.

"You gotta pass him," I say calmly to Little Teena. I look over at Obsidian. She doesn't smile. Smiling's for pussies. I take my sunglasses off and meet my own gaze in the rear view. "Step on it," I go. "We gotta get there first," I say to the rear view mirror. "Park illegally. We have to shadow him when he arrives."

13.

IN THE ER AT THE VIRGINIA MASON CLINIC THERE'S A
dingy fluorescent glow – the pale light of death and the smell
of human fluids mixed with Lysol. The stalls for incoming fucked
people all have sad little blue curtains. Everyone in scrubs is a
trainee. You can just tell. The bags of exhaustion under all their
eyes, the look of maybe going Columbine, the desperate way
they wheel people in and take vitals – somebody's up-all-night
hand shaking with cocaine tremors as they draw blood.

Little Teena's parked his girth at the nurse's desk, making
fictional inquiries about a missing person. Pinned to his
shoulder is an Olympus Mini digital video recorder that looks
pretty much like when cops talk to their shoulders at crime
scenes. One benefit to the Olympus Mini? Its sleek and thin com-
pactness. You'd think they'd be suspicious of him, but they
aren't. The trick is in the details. In the perfect 1970s brown blazer.
And in the ever-so-slightly wrinkled button-down. And the
shit-brown and yellow striped tie. Also, shoes – if you get the
shoes right, people will believe anything. You don't have to be
who you say you are. You only have to be what people have seen
and come to believe on TV. Because we're TV-headed now.

Ave Maria has somehow commandeered a hospital gift shop
cart filled with lame-ola shit. Shampoos and juice boxes. Artifi-
cial flowers and sad-ass balloons on sticks. Stuffed animals and
coffee mugs that say "Get well soon."

I'm in the ER waiting hall on a Naugahyde bench with my

arms crossed over my pink angora chest. My head's down like I'm very, very worried about someone close to me. But really I'm just adjusting the levels of the H4n recorder in my Dora purse.

Obsidian is down the hall a little mopping the floor. Like the Chief in *Cuckoo's Nest*. No one even looks at her. She doesn't even exist. Motherfuckers.

Secured to her wrist watch though is the Aiptek Mini PenCam. Weighing in at only 45 grams and measuring 3 cm × 2.7 cm × 8.6 cm, it's the world's smallest and lightest megapixel digital video recorder. Her head jerks up from mopping and I follow her gaze down the hall.

Our lead actor.

Half walking, half scooting toward the ER incoming desk, comes my man Sig and his member. His head jerks left when two Filipino nurses seem to chuckle. Poor Sig – he has to explain his condition to a none-too-impressed RN dude wearing a crocodile tooth hanging from a chain. Sig's pathetic. He's all bent over. He keeps clearing his throat, gesturing toward the little commandant.

I know what the Sig is thinking though. I do. He's thinking the guy's crocodile tooth is a masculinity talisman. Probably to ward off sexual impotence.

What? I never said I didn't listen.

I whisper, "Tiger One to Bat Boy – over. The chicken is squawking," into my Bluetooth. My voice shoots around the posse. Everyone is in position. Everyone knows exactly who they are. We are our technologies.

Crocodile dude steers Sig to a stall and gives him a hospital smock and a blue blanket to cover himself with – talk about pitching a tent. Jesus. The size of that thing.

The room on the other side of Sig is empty – the gurney all lined up with a shitty-ass hospital pillow waiting for the next victim. I've always hated these rooms. All the save-a-life gadgets and machinery looming above you like you are in the movie *Alien*. I bet it's germ city, too. I know everything is supposed to be all sterilized but I'm guessing it's like a fucking stadium urinal in there. I bet there's dead skin cells and hair and, you know, fluids everywhere. Like in hotel rooms.

The whole place smells like someone shit air freshener.

Ave Maria wheels her cart of fake hope close to Sig's stall. I meet up with Ave Maria and pretend to look at things on the cart, fingering the mugs and stuffed rodents, dabbing my eyes with a tissue.

Crocodile RN then puts an ice-pack on Sig's wang and pushes and says, "Hold that down, sir."

Sig lets out a muffled little yelp.

Various white coats come in and say serious things to Sig. Ask him questions.

At Ave Maria's cart, I put my hand on a mug with a mutant-looking stuffed monkey attached to it. The monkey's head's too big. Like a Down syndrome monkey. Who would feel better if you gave them shit like this?

I point my Dora purse in the direction of Sig's stall. We're all recording – me, Little Teena, Ave Maria, Obsidian. We're transmitting via Bluetooth to the laptop on the floor of the Jag in the parking lot. This, my friends, is how it's done. Quiet on the set.

Three. Two. One. Action.

"Mr. Freud, have you taken any medication for erectile dysfunction?"

"Certainly not," Sig snaps.

White coat nods and asks the same question using different words.

"Do they pay you to be an idiot in training?" Sig blasts.

Oh man. Poor Siggy.

The white coat types information into a computer and talks right over Sig's objections. "Priapism," we hear. "Treated with aspiration. Needle. Penis."

"Fuck me," we hear Little Teena whisper over the Bluetooths. "They're gonna drain his dick!"

I grind my teeth. Then I realize I'm grinding my teeth.

"Let's go over the options, Mr. Freud," the doctor says to the doctor.

It's right about then that a disturbing commotion occurs. Down the hall, shooting straight for us, is an adolescent in a wheelchair. Picking up speed. The closer he gets, the more I see that he's … oh christ. Um, he's, you know, too smiley? Bangs cut too high? Man. What the fuck? Did he escape his keepers? My palms get sweaty. I shake my Farrah head no. This is gonna fuck our shit up.

There's something I have to tell you. When I was in third grade, I was playing four square with the girls in my class, and from way over where the Special Ed kids' classroom was and over into our supposedly normal kids compound – came an adolescent too-smiley. He walked right up to our four square game, all the other girls started shrieking, then he grabbed me, bent me back like in the movies, and French kissed the fuck out of me. It was the most humiliating thing ever. Everyone pointed and ran.

Except me. I bit the inside of my cheek so hard it bled. To this day I have no idea what that was about. But I do know it was intense – what happened between us.

So as bellowing barreling Smiley comes zooming by, getting all up in our scene, I feel a tinge of admiration. Look at him go! Yelling like an idiot. Then I see hospital orderlies in pursuit – but Smiley ditches them and shoots right past us laughing his ass off. We catch each other's eyes for a second, and he winks! I can't help but laugh a little under my breath.

And here come the orderlies, slip slide running after him in aqua-colored scrubs with little booties over their shoes – christ – one of 'em nearly busts his ass rounding the corner.

I mean c'mon. What the hell was that? Close one.

I signal Obsidian to try to mop nearer to Sig. The doctor is saying something about intractable erections when – jesus. Here he comes again! Smiley! He's outsmarted the orderlies in the maze of hospital hallways. I take a closer look at him as he approaches – it's like he's drawn to us like a magnet – like he understands where the action is – some sixth sense in that big old head telling him to run with it. He yells something absolutely incomprehensible. Suddenly I see him differently. He's a rebel without a cause. He's the id unleashed, bringing utter chaos to the pristine pukey halls of an institution.

When he gets to Obsidian – oh jesus. He grabs her ass. With a little yelp and sly smile. I'll be goddamned. He nearly loses his arm when she bats at him with the mop handle. He squawks, but he's still smiling. My man.

Then there's more shouting. Sig bursts out with, "You plan to stab my prick with a giant needle and suck blood, you fucking jackal!" Smiley seems to bellow out a response. The blue blanket of Sig's dignity falls to the floor. I can see Sig's scrawny old-man legs. I can almost see up his hospital gown. Sweat forms on my upper lip and under my boobs and between my ass cheeks. I'm hot. I've got a fucking angora sweater on and this headful of hair – how many pounds does this thing weigh?

Then I hear, "Mr. Freud, have you ingested any narcotics?"

Momentarily, the entire place freezes. Even smiley.

"Fucking get moving you goddamn imbeciles," Sig shouts, breaking the trance, and oh man, then he's really Tourettesing out on them ... more nurses appear outta nowhere.

"Tango One to Tango Two," Ave Maria whispers, "it's *on* ..."

People in Sig's room say things I can't hear. "Everybody move in," I go.

Sig's waving his arms around as Little Teena corners an orderly closer to the scene. He's asking to see a real doctor when Ave Maria pretends her cart is stuck right in front of his drama. And for the briefest of moments, Sig locks eyes with me, the mug with a monkey in my hand. He stops shouting and stares.

Shit. Does he see me?

I point the mug monkey at him and hold my breath. Get well soon.

I have a pop-up thought. See me. These are my eyes. My mouth. I hold the stupid mug out between us.

Mercifully, Smiley yells "GULL" at the top of his lungs, clapping and wheezing wildly, creating a rather magnificent diversion. Saving my ass.

"For christ's sake can someone close the goddamn curtain!" is all Sig says.

Then they close the blue curtain between us.

I shoot Smiley what I hope is a look of sincere gratitude ... he smiles so big it looks like his mouth might split his face.

"I gotta get in there," I whisper-shout up my Bluetooth.

"Are you nuts?" I hear Little Teena growl.

"There's no fucking way I'm missing this, goddamn it," I snap.

Then we all hear a weird whisper-shriek in our ears coming from Ave Maria at her cart. "Use the monkey! Use the monkey! I slit its throat and stuffed a mini spy cam in its head!"

I look down at the mug in my hand. Big-headed monkey. Get well soon. Sure enough, there's a camera lodged in its head, its eye poking out of the deranged monkey mouth. But how to get the thing in Sig's stall? Suddenly it seems obvious.

I look at Smiley.

He looks at me.

We have an unspoken understanding. He wanted in on it from the get-go. He's not fucking up our shit. He's a motherfucking player. I nod at him. His face goes serious and he puts his head forward and clenches his jaw. Faster than you can say "human bomb" I chuck the monkey mug into Smiley's lap. He grips the arms of his wheelchair and puts his head down, ready for action. Orderlies are on the horizon down the hall. I grab the handles of his vehicle and shove his wheelchair as hard as I can until he shoots through the blue curtain right into Siggy's stall.

All hell breaks loose as they try to get the poor kid out of there. But he's playing his part to the hilt – he's shoving the monkey mug at Sig's groin shouting, "Get well soon! Get well soon!" Louder and louder. He's unstoppable. He's beautiful. He's a goddamned natural. One of the nurses tries to get the monkey mug from Smiley but his grip is superhuman. "Get well soon!" he wails.

"Get this moron away from me," Sig screeches, and since the curtain is wide open again I see Sig's hospital gown is all hiked up and there it is – his high-rise wang – looking, I must say, much younger than I expected. Not gray-skinned or wrinkled up at all. Red. Enormous. Monstrously virile. Kinda smells like hot dogs.

My esteemed wheelchair colleague is literally shoving the mug at Sig's dick. But the dick does not yield. Finally a nurse manages to pry the mug loose from his grip. "That's OK now," she's saying to my boy. "Isn't that nice of you," she lies, petting his head. "How thoughtful you are," in the most condescending yet creepily authoritative voice. I briefly consider stabbing her with a fork. Then she wheels my man-boy decoy back out into the hall where the gaggle of orderlies secure their suspect.

Smiley is applauding wildly. What a performance. Fuck it. You gotta give the guy his props. I know it's a risk, but I don't care. I walk straight up to him like I've known him all my fucking life. "Comrade," I announce.

"GULL," he sings up at me.

I raise my hand up in the air in front of him.

He raises his.

I high-five him a hard one, then salute, clicking my heels when I turn to leave.

As I walk away I whisper, "Everybody fall back. Rendezvous at the Jag. Go."

Ave Maria wheels her cart around the corner and abandons it. Little Teena thanks the ER desk ladies for their time. Obsidian rests her mop against a wall and walks away. I stand up and run soap opera dramatic style down the hall like an emotionally distraught woman unable to take it anymore. Wherever they are taking my bellowing lad, at least he had this.

In the parking lot inside the Jag we all four hunch around the laptop, its LCD light glowing up at us. On the screen, Sig's ER room looks fish-eyed and claustrophobic. And you can see some monkey fur around the edges of the shot.

"Fuck almighty," Little Teena says, "it looks like we're looking through a vag."

What we see next is a silver needle that looks big enough to be a rhino tranquilizer gun. The white coat points it at Sig's dinger.

"Good christ," the little cartoon Sig shouts from the computer screen.

"Holy fuck," Obsidian says.

"Youch," Ave Maria says, sticking her hands behind the bib of her candy-striper uniform.

I just feel … itchy. A little like I'm watching a senior shit himself. My upper lip sweats. My head is too heavy with Farrah. And for some weird reason? My twat is throbbing.

When they stick the needle into his cock his face seizes up like his penis might blow fire. I suck in air and clench my hands between my legs. He closes his eyes and groans and sways. He grips the sides of the gurney. The skin of his member is red and purple and swollen. My head hurts. My ears are hot. Sig moans and throws his head back. I see blood suck up the throb of his cock and slowly travel into the hull of the syringe. I pull my hair.

What. The. Fuck. I'm all creamy. Like need a new pair of panties.

The word "shunt" gets batted about by the doctor and nurses. There's a flurry of white as they spring into action. Sig shouts, "Why don't you goddamned medievalists just use leeches?" He's attempting to flee the scene. Blue-suited almost-nurses are holding him down. I realize I'm gripping my own thighs hard enough to leave marks.

"Can you zoom in?" I say, surprised by the coldness of my own voice.

I watch the scalpel inch closer to the head of his penis. As the blade carves a tiny red smile into the tip of his dick, Sig screams bloody murder.

Ave Maria hits a high note.

The urologist gasps.

"FUCK!" I shout.

Sig's cock – I shit you not – shoots blood across the room, a jet of red spraying the white coat of the doctor. A tiny blob of it making it all the way to the monkey camera. Ew.

Now I know why we need the word bellow in the English language, because the sound that comes out of Sig? Bellow.

There is a moment of silence inside the Jag.

"Cut," I say. "Open the goddamn windows." We all take deep breaths.

"Ida," Obsidian goes.

"That's a wrap," I say, rubbing my hands together and wiping sweat off of my upper lip. "Did you guys see that shit? That was some fucked-up shit." My voice sounds a little manic. I've got strange business in my underwear. Ave Maria is rocking and humming "The Star-Spangled Banner," softly.

"Ida," Obsidian repeats.

"Let's blow this pop stand," I say, but Obsidian grabs my head in her hands and points my face toward the window of the Jag. "What?" I say. "We gotta get this footage on a timeline." I notice my voice and hands are shaking.

"Ida," she says, holding my big Farrah head in her hands, and then she gently turns my head and directs my gaze to a man on a gurney being unloaded from an ambulance next to us, "Isn't that your *dad*?"

14.

IT'S HARD TO LOOK AT YOUR DAD WHEN HIS SKIN IS THE color of cigarette ash. It's hard to watch him fighting to breathe right with hospital crap all up his nose and stuck to his face and chest.

Mostly though it's hard to wait the long wait of emergency rooms. There's nothing – and I mean *nothing* – to do. You sit on the shitty-ass Naugahyde chairs and read the shitty-ass *Home Decorating* and *Sailing* and *Newsweek* magazines and watch time stop. The clocks are fucked. They don't move like regular clocks, I swear.

The other people here look like shit on a stick, too. Bags under their eyes and hope shoved a little too high up in their chests. They hold Styrofoam cups of dirt-tasting coffee and wear the same clothes for days. Their hair looks like utter fuck. The women stop wearing make-up and the men stop shaving.

I can see my Farrah wig shoved down into the bottom of my backpack. Mere hours ago I directed the action. Now I just feel about two feet shorter and like my mouth is filled with metal. I think I bit my fucking tongue. Without my Farrah wig, I feel like somebody's lame-ass bald little sister. Christ. I bet they all think I'm a chemo case.

My father's heart attacked him.

I know I'm saying it bassackwards but it seems more honest this way. In a regular heart attack, the blood supply to the heart gets hosed. Heart cells die. In my dad's case, I think there's more to it.

My ass vibrates. It's Little Teena. He texts: *r u ok?* I stare at my iPhone in my hand. My hand is shaking. Great. I'm not even eighteen and I'm already a middle-aged neurotic. I text back: *ok. e.r. sux. need vcdn.*

Emergency rooms. Yeah. I try to remember the layout from earlier. Surely there's a way to score something around here. Where where where did I see the single-dose medicine cabinet?

This waiting room smells like day-old fart. Unfortunately, there's a loser across from me in the waiting room whose coping mechanism is nonstop talking. I cut shapes into the sides of my cup of dirtwater with my fingernails. I try not to clock the ass-wipe across from me blathering on about how his wife wants to raise their kid so much differently than him. His wife he's separated from. Jesus did she make the right move.

"It's about values," comes out of his pie-hole. "You gotta get your kids' minds right early."

This guy wants to send his kid to a Christian Khmer Rouge camp. I swear to god, if there was a god, I'd kick this jack-asstic Christian motherfucker straight in the nuts. But there is no god. If there's anything, it's an anti-god. With a very perverse sense of humor.

I'd go back in to see my dad but I have to do it in little doses. It makes me feel like crap. The sounds of hospital gadgets. The smell of beating back death. Besides, his head looks weird all hooked up to hospital crap.

I'M SIX.

I am with my father at the edge of an estuary that is a bird sanctuary. Marshlands and birch and ferns stretch out before us, divided by small cool streams weaving through grasses and sand.

My father reaches into his brown brushed-corduroy father pants that smell like Irish Spring soap and Good Life cologne – a sharp spicy amber fragrance that lends itself to a blend of citrus, lavender, sweet spices, and sandalwood I know from reading the label in his man bathroom when he's not there – he reaches into his pocket and pulls something out and says, "I have a present for you."

My father gives me a Kodak Instamatic camera. I know because he puts his father pointer finger under each word and then we say the words together: "Kodak. Instamatic. Camera."

"This is not a toy," he says to me, and he puts the yellow and black box with red and blue writing on it and a tiny black eye into the smallness of my hands. I feel very serious. Or I try to.

This is how you hold it up and look through the little viewing square.

This is how you pan for the shot – you want to pretend you are making a box around what you see – that's how the picture will turn out.

This is the button you push to take the shot – here – listen – hear the "click?"

Then after, this is how you advance the film – see this little dial – you put your thumb on it like this – you try it – yes, like that, and keep rolling it forward until it stops.

Then you are ready for your next picture.

They are instructions. Suddenly I want him to say them all over again. Again. Again. Ordering the world.

He squats down even lower so that he's kid eye level and I hold the camera up to my eye and he reaches his long father arm out before us toward the land and says, "OK, now you can choose for yourself what to shoot."

"Shoot?" I say, dropping the camera down.

"Take a picture. It means take a picture."

I turn toward him and point my head and the camera right at him and he starts to laugh and he says, "No, Ida, you can take a picture of ANYTHING out here, not me, not me ..." but I take pictures of him laughing, of his ear, of his chin. His eye and the top of his head. His shoes. Now we are both laughing.

Then he picks me up and puts me up on his shoulders and says, "OK, OK," and still kind of laughing he says, "Shoot."

I do. I shoot everything in the whole world.

A LOT HAS happened since I was six.

I wish my dad's head would look normal again is all.

My cell vibrates. Ave Maria. *hwz ur dad?* How is he? I stand up to go check. My head swims. I sit back down and grip my iPhone. *Alive* I text. Then I see a flash of beige.

My mother hovers into my father's room like a ghost. Even I can barely tell when she's there, when she's not. She wears off-white pants and a blond sweater. Trust me when I say she blends in with the earth-toned décor. I shadow her. I stand just outside his stall, out of view. She doesn't say anything to him. She leans over close to his face like she's going to softly pet his skin or kiss him. But she doesn't do either. She just leans in close to his face and closes her eyes, then presses the sides of her hair back.

I'M TWELVE.

The front door of the condo opens and there is a tree with white flowers standing there. No, it's my father coming home from work with an armful of lilies for my mother. He peeks around the ginormous bouquet and he is smiling. He is smiling so big his face looks weird.

She is not.

She has been running the back of her hand over the keys of the baby grand she has not played for years. In her other hand is a scotch on the rocks. Which to me has become one word: scotchontherocks.

His happiness lives in his pants.

Briefly I wonder if he smells like Mrs. K. in his pants. The lilies scent obliterates anything.

I'm in the kitchen getting a Coke. I can see them through the kitchen door opening in the living room. His happy head pushes the enormous bouquet of sickeningly sweet-smelling flowers all up into her face.

She embraces them like she might a child, and for a second, I think I see color back in her eyes. The corner of one side of her mouth twitches briefly. I'm standing there riveted, my Coke midair, my mouth hanging open, watching the scene of them.

It's wrong.

His happy head.

Pants.

It's his pleasure that's the death of her.

Slowly, like as slowly as twelve-year-old possible, I slide my iPhone out from my back pocket with my free hand. I lift it up, set it to film, aim it at them. But twelve-year-olds are gawky and awkward, so my mother sees me move out of the corner of her eye just as I hit the little red record button.

"Ida, don't," she says, holding the giant flowers in front of her head.

Then she sort of "flees" – runs out of the frame. Room I mean. In my hand she looks like a woman with a floral head where her human head should be, dashing to safety. I hear the bedroom door close from down the hall.

Then it's just my father and the scent of something too sweet still lingering in the room.

Like childhood.

I GO BACK to the room where people wait for bad shit to happen. Jeez.

The weirdest part though is that Mrs. K. is here too. She makes sure to go into his room when my mother is not there, when my mom is down getting some godforsaken fake food from the cafeteria or going for a walk down the maze of hospital hallways. What, is she casing the joint? I can't figure out where she's hiding out. Visually though, she's pretty much the opposite of my mom. Mrs. K. has flaming red hair. A lot of it. Like mythic. Mrs. K. has a full, round, heart-shaped ass. My mom's ass slid down her hamstrings years ago. Mrs. K. has big tits – like 1950s big tits. My mom's tits are slowly attempting to hide in her armpits like frightened fried eggs.

My mom knows Mrs. K. is there. She does. But she has so perfected her denial that she can go deaf and blind at a moment's notice. If I think about all this much longer I'm going to barf in the lap of Christian blabberpuss. I watch my mother walk right past me and down one of the halls Smiley so recently travelled. I hope he takes care of her.

OF COURSE the Sig scene is in my head. By now he's probably home vacuum-breathing a table full of blow to ease his wang pain. To be honest? I kind of wish I was with him. How weird is that?

Dirtwater coffee suddenly soaks my crotch. I cut a fingernail chimp face in the Styrofoam cup and now it's everywhere. Christianpiehole stops talking for a second, looks at my wet crotch, smiles, then continues. All Christians are pervs.

Kind of I can't breathe. Hospital air – did you know it's all "contained" in the compound? There's no such thing as fresh air in the compound. It's recirculated and sterilized. Like in a spaceship. I make a break for the stairwell and the red letters of an exit sign. I stand on a little platform between floors outside and try to breathe like a normal fucking person. I close my eyes. For some goddamn reason I flash on an image of Mrs. K.'s luminous big ass. Briefly it seems light and easy to jump. Which makes me feel more dizzy. I slap my cheek as hard as I can. Youch. That'll wake you up in the morning. Then I try to smile/grimace like a chimp.

That's when I have my epiphany. The sick daughter has a sick father, who has a sick mistress, who has a sick husband, who jumps the bones of the sick daughter.

That's not the epiphany.

I re-enter the hospital compound. The meds in lots of ER areas are in a special cabinet containing medication bins and refrigerators that store limited quantities of medications in single-unit containers. You'd be surprised how often those cabinets and fridges are unattended. I mean it's a busy place, the ER. So hijacking Vicodin is a piece of cake. Particularly if you have a Swiss Army knife special edition. One thing I'm good at.

After pocketing the velvet, I go into my father's room. He looks dead. But he doesn't sound dead. His breathing is what they call shallow and labored. Goddamn it, why are dads such a big fucking *deal*?

Me and my father in a room that smells like hand sanitizer and plastic barf bags. Before I realize what I'm doing I pull my Zoom H4n outta my Dora purse. Before I can stop myself I place it close to his face. Turn it on. Adjust the levels.

"Dad?" I go.

Just the sound of him breathing, amplified, recorded. Sounds … kind of like a horse. Some kinda fist swells up in my throat and my eyes itch. I stare at the H4n. Its glowing LCD display. Its two silver criss-crossing mics. The only other thing I know how to do. Way more than knowing how to be a daughter. I walk away. Why the hell am I holding my breath?

I can still hear Christianmouth going. I look down the hall to the right. No one. I look to the left. Nothing. Everything smells like day-old Lysol and medicine.

My ass vibrates again. Obsidian. She texts: *wnt 2 c u*. My throat constricts. I close my eyes. Then and only then do I cry. Like a pussy. I hold the phone of her against my cheek. Some jackass in scrubs asks me if I'm OK and I nearly backhand him with the H4n and snarl at him with my chimp face.

The idiotic fluorescent lights buzz down on my head. I feel alone and stupid. I want to sprint down one of these fucked-up hallways, find smiley. I want to put my face in Obsidian's hair. I want to press all of my skin onto all of her skin. But I'd just pass out. Wouldn't I?

This is the epiphany: there's no mother here. She's not there to say, hey Christian fuck, that's my daughter. She doesn't want to hear about your shitty-ass parenting skills. Her father just had a massive coronary and open heart surgery. Shove your-self up your own ass.

She's not here to tell Mrs. K., that's my husband, ho bag. Step back before I irradiate you with my voice.

She's not here to make chimp faces with me.

I run as hard and loud as I can all the way down to the big red-letter exit sign. I look up. I open my mouth. "Are you my mother?" is what I try to say out loud. But nothing comes out.

I cough. An odd sound strangles my throat.

It's my voice.

She's gone.

15.

I'M GROUNDED AGAIN. IT'S A LITTLE ABSTRACT AS TO why. Whatever.

At home, in my room, I write on the walls with my purple Sharpie underneath my Nico poster: "Dear Francis Bacon: I don't want to talk anymore since that's not what mouths are for. I know a mouth is not a mouth. In your paintings? All the mouths are smeared senseless." I cap my pen. I put it in my backpack.

I have a Swiss Army knife. The "Elite," custom-made. It even has a cigar-cutter. I stole it from Mr. K. a year ago. I pull it out of my backpack. I open up two of the blades. I lie on my bed as still as a dead girl. I close my eyes. I run the blades over my stomach slowly and softly. It's relaxing. I can cut a new mouth any-where on my body I want. My gut. My collarbone. My bicep. My thigh.

I pull out the cigar-cutter. All I see is Sig.

Approximately one quarter of all myocardial infarctions are silent, without chest pain or other symptoms. Apparently that's what happened with my dad. My mom says he came home from work that night, mixed a highball, loosened his tie, greeted her, walked into the living room, put on some Thelonious Monk, and in slow motion, "like he deflated," sank to the floor. They say his attack happened earlier in the day. That was just his body finally answering.

They moved my dad to a normal room, though he's still hooked up to creepy shit. My dad is in and out. When he sees my mom, he stares at her face, then looks away and goes to sleep. When he sees me, his eyes are all glassy. I can see two Ida heads in his peepers. It's creepy and usually it makes me have to pee. We don't stay long.

Earlier today at the hospital I heard Mrs. K.'s laughter coming out of his room. So I guess he's getting better. Her laugh sounds like ... happy opera. It makes me happy and sad and pissed off all at the same time.

My bed smells like teen spirit. I open my eyes. I look at the cracks in my ceiling. Then I pull up my shirt and look down at my belly. Stretched between my hipbones my belly looks like an awesome skateboard bowl. I lift my shirt up more and I cut a very straight line just under my rib cage on the right side. I can feel the crimson line of it coming to life under my fingertips. It's not smiling.

Now that I'm thinking about it, my mother didn't actually say, "You are grounded." What she said was, "The trauma of the current situation trumps your little shenanigans and your hoodlum friends." It sounded icy. I think that voice kills hair and skin cells – like radiation. Because we rarely speak? She's totally indifferent to my voice situation. Actually I don't even think she knows. Isn't that something? I suppose I could text her, but really, why? My silence? It's what's kept the house in order.

I'm a little concerned, however. All the times before, I was faking it. Using losing a voice when I needed it. Mostly anyway. Except for that time at the lake with Mr. K. when he jammed his cow tongue down my throat and I had to knee him in the nads. It's been five days since my voice left. There isn't really anything to "do" about it.

Well, OK, that's a lie. It might be that there is someone who could help me get it back ... I have a new empathy for that little stuck cuckoo in Sig's clock. Fat chance now though, huh?

By now he's figured out I'm the one who pumped him up with Viagra and cocaine. He's a smart old guy. Probably it's over between us, is my guess. Probably that matters but all I feel is a welcoming sting under my rib. I suck my fingers and taste metal.

At ten o'clock my iPhone vibrates. Everyone's meeting at Marlene's. I pack my backpack and climb out of my window and down the fire escape as the last little tinkling sounds of ice cubes in a drink fade out. Mother's self-medicating big time. As am I. Mostly Xanax.

You know the first uses of Xanax were for panic disorders. The first pharmaceutical company to produce Xanax was Upjohn. Upjohn – isn't that a hoot? Upjohn? I mean, did no one think of the connotations? The real name is Alprazolam. Which sounds like Flash Gordon or some superhero name. You know who told me all that? Sig. Why do I keep thinking of him? Is this weird hole in my throat me missing him? Fuck. Just shoot me.

At the bottom of the fire escape I try to clear my head with dumb thoughts. My favorite idiotic drug name is Aciphex. Say it out loud few times. Endless fun.

I can't tell you how much better I feel when I'm not in the Nazi daughter box – our so-called home. Ten o'clock at night in downtown Seattle is über cool. Everything looks the color of a bruise. The storefronts and restaurants are rows of little well-lit caves. Every alley smells like pee, but it's a familiar smell. A downtown smell. Smells like life. Sometimes you can hear the clopping of horse cop hooves. I hustle it down a few blocks to the 7-Eleven and buy a Pez dispenser with the head of Ernie from Ernie and Bert. You know, *Sesame Street*. When I leave the store I chuck the Pez and fill the dispenser with the Vicodin I lifted from the ER. They fit perfectly. It's awesome. Obsidian showed me that. I put the Ernie-headed Pez in my Dora purse.

The posse meets up at Marlene's for a junk exchange – and to hang out. I think they are trying to take care of me. You know, like a family would. If families existed. I guess they're all pretending they have a sad little mute friend.

Eight blocks, three homeless people, and a horse cop giving a frat boy a drunk walk-the-line test later, I make it to Marlene's.

When she opens the door, I smile. A lot. In fact I nearly bawl smiling. You haven't lived until you've seen Marlene in her Scarlett O'Hara green vintage velvet dress. With fan.

"Lamskotelet!" she says, quivering her fan.

Fiddle-dee-dee.

Inside of Marlene's apartment it's us. Me, Ave Maria, Little Teena, and Obsidian, who is sitting on the kitchen counter. I can't help it. All I see is Obsidian. Obsidian's jeans have the knees worn out of them and her skin is brown as fine Albuquerque dirt. Her white T-shirt creeps up her biceps kinda James Dean-like. Her black hair … blows the word "night" away. There's not a guy on earth who could be more pussy-whipped by this girl than I am. I lift up my shirt. She looks at my new little expression-less mouth. She smiles. She licks her lips.

Marlene as Scarlett makes us all mint juleps. We spread our junk out on her kitchen table and divvy it up. I throw my Ernie down and a few Xanax.

That's not all we throw down on the kitchen table. We throw down high-capacity SD memory cards. Terabyte portable hard drives the size of little wallets. All the recorded junk from the Sig scene. We stare at the table. No one says anything. No one asks about my dad, thank fuck. I collect all the recorded crap and shove it into my backpack and zip it as fast as humanly pos-sible. I texted them all before I got there. *No voice.* They've been through it with me before. They know not to joke. But they look so serious. When I look around at everyone? I make a chimp face. Everyone laughs.

"I got a month-long gig with the ivories at Tula's on Sundays at four p.m.," Little Teena announces.

"Tula's – is that the one with Mediterranean food?" Ave Maria asks. "I think my mom took me there. I think we heard Sax Attack Quartet or some shit there. My mom got loaded and they called a cab."

Obsidian laughs – but her laugh is a low roll that sounds like she's always high or wise. "Sax Attack Quartet? Is that real?"

I want to say, "That sounds just like Aciphex," and then we'd all laugh, but I can't.

"Tula's!" Marlene says with a thick southern belle voice – "Wynton Marsalis once said 'This is a cool place' about that place!"

I always knew Little Teena's fingers would take him someplace someday. He's actually an astonishing pianist. Once my mom heard him play on our now-silent baby grand and she put her hand on his shoulder like he was the son she never laid. For her? That was deep affection. Or artistic respect. Or something. I keep hoping his hands will take him into another world.

I risk moving across the kitchen closer to Obsidian. I brace myself on the counter on the other side of the sink from where she perches and inch my ass over toward her. So far, so good. I stare at her knees. Kind of I want to suck on them.

You know, when you can't talk, talking sounds different. Everyone sounds like a soundtrack of talking instead of like people. Maybe without a voice you're hyper-attuned to listening or something. But it's like there's a distance between you and everyone's talking – like they are on a stage and you are in the audience – and all their voices suddenly sound … like art. It's comforting.

Ave Maria talks about missing her fourteenth, fifteenth, sixteenth day of school.

Little Teena talks about Hitchcock movies and Jimmy Stewart.

Obsidian says her uncle is in jail for beating the crap out of his brother's wife.

"Harsh," Ave Maria goes, and we all sip mint juleps while Obsidian punches her own bicep. It makes a rhythmic thud. Like a slow heart.

I don't know why she does that but it's mesmerizing.

Then, Marlene waves her fan in a great sweeping gesture collecting all our attention and suggests we watch *Gone with the Wind* on Blu-ray in the living room.

I don't say a word. I'm the hearer. The listener. The recorder.

I inch a little closer to Obsidian. I can feel my butt getting wet from the edge of Marlene's sink as I make my way over but I don't care. I can smell her skin. She smells like rain. I want to climb her and grind her right there on the counter. Then I realize I'm close enough to touch because she puts her hand on my hand and momentarily I go blind. Deaf. Whatever. I don't care. I surrender. Maybe I'll just crack my skull open on the floor and not have to think anymore. I send up a silent wish to not god, but to Francis Bacon. I brace myself to black out and fall to the floor. I close my eyes and think about silent heart attacks – how loving someone could deflate you until you fell to the floor. I shut my eyes and hold my breath.

But you know what happens?

Obsidian puts her knees up in my armpits and shoots her legs out so I am sorta hanging on her like a rag doll.

"Dora, honey?" I hear Little Teena's voice.

"Liebchen?" Marlene goes, skirt rustling nearer.

I hear too a little soft coo high note in the background.

Then not god, but Francis Bacon gives me shoulder pads. No; it's Obsidian. She's got her hands on my shoulders. I open my eyes. She's staring straight into me. I don't faint. She carefully slides down from the kitchen counter and hugs me. I put my arms around her neck. I put my face in her hair. I can smell rain. I don't faint. I pull back. She smiles. I've never seen her smile like this. It's a smile you can feel since before you were born. Up close? Her eyes aren't brown like I always thought they were. There are little flecks of green in them, like a gem that turns colors only in certain light.

"You're OK," she says to me.

The "OK" rings in my head like art.

Then, with her arm around my waist, we follow Marlene's voice into the living room to watch *Gone with the Wind* on Blu-ray like it's the most normal thing in the universe.

I mouth the words *fuck yeah*. And smile.

There's no father here. No mother. It's like you can erase your origins and be anybody else.

"Tomorrow is anothah day," Marlene sings, way cooler than Vivien Leigh.

16.

JUST WHEN YOU THINK THINGS ARE AS CLUSTERFUCKED as they can get, they fuckgasm straight out of orbit.

Yeah. Mr. and Mrs. K.? Turns out, they have kids. Two vile midget creatures. I swear they have fur on their paws. Wanna know how I know? They're *here*. At the condo. The boy creature is trying to get a Tetra – those bullshit blue and red fish everyone on the planet has in their aquarium because they live and die quickly and flush easily – out of the aquarium with one of my mother's beloved spoons, while the girl creature – what is up with that hair? Who puts a ponytail straight up on the top of a kid head? She looks like Cindy Lou Who. Only uglier. She stares at me. Picks her little creature snot nose. Throws it at me. Charming.

Because my dad's at home recuperating. Because Mrs. K. is "helping out." Because my mother? You're gonna love this. Apparently, now is the optimum supremo cool time to *go stay with her great aunt in Vienna*.

I know. I can't believe it either. Vienna? Seriously? Hello, but don't you have a spare DAUGHTER lying around the house? All I got was a shitty-ass note on the baby grand that said "Ida, you are certainly old enough to take care of yourself for a while. A nurse from the hospital will visit once a day. Your father has plenty of help. He needs peace and quiet. Be mature. This is a difficult time. Don't get in the way."

Awesome. You know, I'd be crushed and all, but the more I'm around this family, the more I understand – things must always get worse, or the drama goes impotent. That's the fucked-up part about life. You have to keep stroking the family drama. Wouldn't want anyone to feel, you know, good about their lives or selves exactly the way they are. Wouldn't want any bullshit Zen calm descending on the home. That'd be nuts. You stroke the drama with everything you've got until you run out of energy. Then you die. The end. Orgasm accomplished.

Goddamn god. Or anti-god.

Just look at those midgets. I walk over to the she-midget. I give her a little kick. She falls over and her face gets red like she's gonna cry. Oh, but she doesn't cry. She's a crafty little midget. She licks the toe of my Doc, then looks up at me like that sly nasty Chucky elf dude in the horror flicks. Great. Our house is now possessed by short pudgy demons.

The boy creature flips the Tetra straight over his shoulder with the spoon. I stare at it on the floor there for a second. Wriggling. Helpless. Out of its element. What's the best option? Smash it into the carpet with my foot, or carefully return it to the tank? Does it really matter?

I choose the latter. But not because I'm any kind of savior. Frankly I feel a tinge of guilt – here, little guy, here you go back into your idiotic fake water prison with plastic plants and colored rocks and oh! A creepy miniature scuba dude! I'll be in Vienna!

The door to my father's bedroom down the hall opens. I can hear her before I see her. The happy opera laugh. Then it's that mythic mane of deep-red hair and lips to match and ta-tas all up high and bouncing under a hunter-green sweater. Then I get an extra treat. Boompappy. She turns and bends over to pick up a pearl drop earring from the carpet. Her ass fills the hall and blurs out all the surrounding setting. Thank you Francis Bacon for that beautiful ass shot. I bite the inside of my own cheek as punishment.

I should hate this woman.

Slut.

Ho.

Adulterer.

Homewrecker.

Instead I want to go make a series of T-shirts with each of those words on them and graphic drawings of her stripped naked. What? How should I know why?

I really do need to get some professional help.

Except I clusterfucked that one up myself.

Mrs. K. walks down the hall toward me. She passes right by her own children like they are furniture. Bigger and bigger she gets. Like in a movie close-up. My head itches. I'm actually growing hair. Then she's right in front of me. She smells like Hypnose. Made by Lancôme. Paris. A captivating fragrance for a charming woman with an intriguing attitude. It's the same stuff Marlene wears. Goddamn it.

What I want to say is, "Um, this is pretty uncomfortable. Can I go stay with my friends for a while?" What I'm afraid I'll say is, "Can I lift up your skirt and maybe sink my teeth into your big white ass? Just a little?" But I got no voice. So I stand there like an idiot with my hands dangling from my arms like big useless spoons. My mouth hanging open. I try to close it casually.

Mrs. K. brushes a lock of hair away from her cheek and says, "Ida, be a dear, will you, and watch the children while I go get your father some medicine?"

No shit.

I look over at the creatures. Now I'm a babysitter? I wonder briefly what it would be like to sit on 'em till they pass out.

But it doesn't end there. As she's walking out the door?

"Oh, and Mr. K. will be by later to take you and the children out for dinner. Isn't that nice?"

The door to my own home closes behind her. I feel a low rage boiling up from my ribcage. I stare down the hall to where my father is needing his peace and quiet. Peace and quiet? Is that what he needs? Really? Is that what he gave us? I look at the two kid lumps I've been left to command. I steer them toward the kitchen, where I literally give them a bowl of sugar cubes.

They smack their evil demon midget gums and laugh. Their eyes immediately get shiny. I shake my head up and down and smile. Good, isn't it. Have another.

Then my ass vibrates. At first I just let it … I mean, who cares, right? I'm stuck here at least until Mrs. K. gets her big beautiful whore ass back. But then I go ahead and look.

Holy shit.

Holy, motherfucking, shit. I know that number.

Though no one but a couple of sugar-dosed cretins sees it, I click my heels together. I salute the empty air. "Herr Doktor!" I go.

In my head, I mean.

Fuck. He can't hear me.

"Hello," I hear him say. "Ida? Are you there? I very much need to speak with you. Is this Ida?"

I look around the room for something to make noise with. Just the evil midgets. I stare at the phone. I put it back to my ear and breathe as hard as I can as loud as I can. Fuck. I sound like a prank caller – but it's all I've got.

"Ida?" Sig says. His voice all small and electronic. I scan the room. THE SPOON. I snatch the spoon out from the grip of the boy creature. I tap the spoon on the iPhone in a little rhythm – twinkle twinkle little star. What? It's the first thing that occurred to me. I pause, and wait, and hold my breath.

"Tap once if this is Ida," Sig says. I told you he was smart.

I tap once.

"Tap twice if you can meet me tomorrow at 4:00. Your regular time. It is imperative that we meet. I think … I think you know why."

I think about it.

"Shall I take your silence as a 'no?'" Sig responds.

I tap twice. So hard it cracks the plastic on the front of the iPhone.

"Until then," Sig says.

I look at Mrs. K.'s creatures. Their faces are blotchy. Sugar high kicking in. Pretty soon they'll rock 'n' roll. In my ear is the voice of the man whose dick I just filmed being drained. In my mouth is the spoon used in a previous murder attempt on a Tetra fish. I suck it. Tastes like fish. Or girl.

17.

THE BASIC METHODOLOGY FOR EDITING VIDEO AND audio is to highlight the clip and drag it onto the timeline. My studio is in a corner of my bedroom where I built a false wall made from two-by-fours and old record album covers. Mostly I used a staple gun to build the false wall. You don't need a darkroom to edit video or audio, but it's cooler to work in the dark. I don't know why that is. When I'm in there though, there is no trespassing. Once my dad tried to come in there and I missed his thigh by inches with the staple gun. In my studio, everything is MINE.

You can use the above method for as many clips as you want. If you want to trim your clips, you select a clip and double-click it. In the viewer window, you have play controls. You can press play, scrub frame by frame, you can click the jog wheel and move shit around. You can drag and drop clips, trim them, close gaps between clips, add effects like fade-ins and fade-outs and cross-fades and crap. Those are the basic ways for editing clips on a timeline in Final Cut Pro.

The in and out points on your timeline are crucial.

In between feeding Mrs. K.'s evil midgets sugar cubes and sticks of butter, I compile the Sig footage. If all goes well they'll be shitting their pants by the time Mrs. Prima Donna K. gets back and I can get the fuck outta here down the fire escape. My plan is to have a rough cut of the film ready by tonight – I've arranged for a small group of trusted brilliant scruffy teens to meet up with me and the posse. At the Fremont troll statue under the north end of the Aurora Bridge. Midnight. I need an audience test – a preview sneak peek – to see if I'm on the right track. All serious filmmakers do it.

The girl gremlin lets out a long gurgly fart that I can hear all the way from the living room. She babbles, "Poo poo in the potty?" Right on schedule. Shouldn't be long now.

I'm concerned about the narrative arc of the film. I decided not to go chronologically … yeah, I know, that's gonna throw some viewers off, but it seemed like the most obvious choice, so I abandoned it immediately. Besides, who wants to watch a movie of a middle-aged man scoring a boner and then needing medical attention? I'm a professional. I went with kind of a more Maya Deren approach – more surrealism than realism. More symbolic. More like how dreams are.

Maya Deren's real name was Eleanora Derenkowsky. Ukrainian. Her father was a psychiatrist who worked at the State Institute for the Feeble-Minded in NYC. Her mother was an artist. Lucky duck. She was a leading avant garde filmmaker. Well except that she was next to invisible because she was a woman. Of course I learned this from Marlene, who showed me *Meditation on Violence* when I was fourteen.

"Experiment with the effects contemporary technical devices have on nerves, minds, or souls." Yep, Maya Deren said that. I dig it. She also said: "I make my pictures for what Hollywood spends on lipstick." Fuck yeah.

So for example, in my film, there are slow-motion shots of the Sigster's wang getting bigger and bigger in between repeated images of him drinking tea. Or petting the spines of his books in his bookcase. Faster and faster. Sip tea sip tea WANG. Pet books pet books sip tea WANG. Like that. I'm thinking of laying down some speeded-up Vivaldi.

I magnified the bit where the scalpel actually cuts into Sig's dong footage. At first hard to tell what you are seeing. Gradually as I pull the view back you understand what you are looking at. When his dong shoots blood – I use time-lapse. You've seen time-lapse photography. Cloudscapes and celestial motion. Plants growing and flowers opening. Fruit or road kill rotting. The evolution of a construction project. People in a city. Or, the enormous dong of Sig shooting blood across the room. I set a background behind it of – what else? Cuckoo clocks and cuckoos cuckooing their heads off.

But I don't want it to be the kind of film you have to be super high on acid to understand. Or the kind of art you have to read books about to get. I don't want it to draw the Seattle nerd wannabe art boys with plaid shirts and odd coifs. I'm no Gus Van Sant.

No, it's not a movie about some crusted old guy who gets a boner.

Sig and his sausage? He's just a man-symbol. It's a movie about everything. This world we live in. The bodies we're stuck with. The lives we get whether we want them or not. How hard you have to work just to get through a fucking day without killing yourself.

And how girls are virtually invisible. How that will be in the movie is me splicing in shots of Billie Holiday. Heidi. Nico. Maya Deren. You get the picture.

Technically I haven't laid down the sound yet. But I've got buttloads of cool shit to work with. Sometimes I think the sound is more important than the images. Like giving the images … I don't know, life.

The boy creature in the living room yells, "BOOOOOMER." I smell shit.

I burn a copy of the video footage for transport. I'm thinking he's crapped himself.

I hear the return of Mrs. K. to the condo.

I hear her say, "Oh!" And call out, "Ida!" And, "Ida?" And, "What on earth? What is all this butter?"

That's my cue. I gather up my stuff and head out the

fire escape toward the posse and the troll statue. I blow a kiss in the direction of Mrs. K. and her two steaming little piles of shit.

Babysitter my ass.

18.

ANY SUCCESSFUL FILMMAKER TESTS A ROUGH CUT TO gauge the interaction between the art and the audience. I wouldn't say I let that reaction prescribe what I do next, but I do like to get a sense of it – in case I want to further fuck with their comfort levels or expectations. Art is a verb.

I stage a showing at midnight underneath the Fremont bridge near the troll. I project it straight onto the cement wall. At midnight. Gathered are a gaggle of punksters and hipsters and young rebel hoodlums. It's like a black skinny jeans and Emo haircut convention. It smells like pot and vodka and clove cigarettes – like someone exploded a cinnamon molotov cocktail. Little Teena sets down a cooler full of Guinness. Ave Maria passes out Percocet. Obsidian helps me get the sound levels right.

The CTA Digital LT-PP Projector with iPhone cable is a portable solution for displaying movies up to eighty-six inches in size. It supports digital files from its SD card reader. It can run for short amounts of time on a rechargeable lithium-ion battery. It's beyond awesome.

When everyone has a spot to sit in the dirt or lean on a rock or tree or car, I start her up. For some reason I've always liked the dumb black and white old-school numbers on a target intro of five. Four. Three. Two. One. Beep. Makes it feel real.

The first image is so bright everyone shields their eyes briefly. Like a white explosion. It's because the film opens with a field of snow. Mounds of it. As you are trying to figure out more about the setting, the camera pulls back and a gritty electronic soundscape kicks in and the more the camera pulls back the more you realize you are looking at *snow*, not snow. Booger sugar on a mahogany table.

There are many reasons I chose that as the opening image. But the main reason is this: I see my man Sig's cocaine use as symbolic of both a strength and a weakness. On the one hand, what the fuck is a doctor doing hopping up on blow and then pretending to "heal" people? And why does the pharmaceutical industrial complex and its army of bourgeois users get a get-out-of-jail-free card while we fill up prisons with uneducated poor folks?

On the other hand, name your top five favorite musicians of all time. Or artists. Or scientists. Now name their vices. Uh huh. What would culture be without drugs? I'll tell you what. Sad sack of shit is what. It's just a paradox.

So the visual metaphor of blow is important as an opening metaphor.

The next few image sequences are a quickly moving collage of Siggy popping in and out of his office mixed with speeded-up downtown bum scenes, stock footage of experimental monkeys with electrodes in their heads and needles in their guts, extreme close-ups of cigars or cuckoo clocks with mangled birds or black leather, a big hand tapping a pencil on a desk, nuclear explosions and Hiroshima burned up folks, that type deal. Bitchin' soundscape and music. Then the collage sort of breaks apart into abstract fragments sort of like a broken mirror, until the fragments become two buffalos fucking. Zoom in on the male buffalo humping away – its eyes rolling back.

Cue the Wagner.

Cut to Siggy losing his shit in his office. Cut to his big dong taking over the story. All of it in s l o w m o t i o n .

By the time he's launching himself into the cab he looks monstrous. I love how slow motion close-ups do that. I've got his

voice slowed down too, so all the tourettesing out sounds like …
demons. It's just creepy as shit.

Then I go back to an overwhelming whiteness – only this
time it's institutional – and as things come into focus you see
you are in a hospital. From there, well I guess you know what from
there. Sig and his wang-shooting-blood scene right at the
Wagner crescendo. Only I also splice in little shots of gigantic
zoomed-in women's breasts, twats, and asses. So devouring and
huge they could swallow a human head. Like Godzilla-sized tits
and vag. Like anti-porn. I get a standing ovation.

I bow and chuckle and shake my head. That little stuffed
monkey cam? Golden.

When it's all over we mill about and drink all the beer up
and laugh and shoot the shit. People drift over my way one, two,
three at a time and give me ideas and reactions. Most of them
are media savvy and, well I don't know if you know this, but we're
all of us film experts without ever having had to receive special
educations. It's the dominant reality of our lives. The moving
image. We were born with it. It's our generation's lexicon. You are
already behind.

At about two a.m., me, Ave Maria, Little Teena and Obsidian
decide to go out. I pocket the SD card with the film on it and
stow the mini projector in the trunk of Ave Maria's mom's Jag.
Everyone has a fake ID thanks to Little Teena. If you must know,
we've had them since we were fourteen. He just revises them
as we age. It's not as fun passing as it used to be though now because, well, we look older. We look adultish. It's kind of a drag.
We make our way to Rebar.

The first thing I notice once we're inside is that Ave Maria
has shaved off her eyebrows. I don't know why the fuck I didn't
see it over at the troll but now it's plain as day. I lean over and
point to her eyebrows and tilt my head in question. She smells
like candy. The music pounds up through my heels and shins and
knees from the floor.

She spins around and shouts inexplicably at the top of

her lungs, "Look at my bitchin' brow bone!" For a moment she looks like a punk neanderthal. She smiles big as a candy-apple-headed girl ape and twirls away.

I sip on a vodka and grapefruit and people-watch. Just a sea of dancing bodies. Colors shooting from lights all over the room. Hair. Just sweat and synthetic clothing and cool shoes. Then I close my eyes. I let the bass thud thought out of my skull. I let the music remember me as a body. I let a rhythm release me from a self. Pretty soon I'm dancing and rubbing and grinding with other bodies all around me. Only there's no me. I laugh and jump up and down and dance. Manic. Good manic. Wouldn't that be something? To get to be a not-me all the time? I catch glimpses of the posse or we dance together and then separate.

There is no other I than them.

When I'm sopping wet I decide to rehydrate. I take off my Velvet Underground T-shirt and stuff it partly into my back jeans pocket. I'm glad I wore my black Lycra bra and not my little red push-up because the little red push-up sometimes exposes a nip when I wish it wouldn't. I stomp back over to the bar. While I'm waiting for my drink, I see something out of the corner of my eye. Like a glint of silver. I look to my left, and there's a hot-looking older dude sitting at a little table with two people my age – one male, one female. The male looks feminine and the female looks butch. The attractive older dude smiles at me. I smile at him. He's way good-looking. Kind of in that David Bowie way. The dude never ages, you know? Makes my mouth water. This guy's like that. It's hard not to look at him.

In fact, it's like he's got a tractor beam. He's locked on. I feel magnetically pulled over to the table. The boy who looks like a girl parts his chin-length bangs and smiles. The girl who looks like a boy crosses her bare arms and her biceps bulge and she smiles. The hot older dude nods his head yes. Before I know it I'm stomping straight up to them.

I can smell patchouli, but I've no idea which one of them

is wearing it. Patchouli has this weird way of making me drowsy and yes-y. Like catnip.

The attractive older dude says, "Won't you join us?"

The boygirl and the girlboy's heads bob in agreement. They slide over on their shared red vinyl booth seat and make a spot for me. I don't know why, but it seems like I fit in there.

I flash them a peace sign and sit down and sip my drink.

"I'm Otto," the boygirl goes.

"I'm Sabina," the girlboy goes.

I smile. I sip my drink. I rummage around in my Dora purse and pull out my purple Sharpie and write on my drink napkin – wait – who am I again? Oh yeah. I write "DORA". They all smile and nod. I look at attractive older dude. That's when it dawns on me. I've SEEN him before. At the restaurant. He's the guy who made Siggy faint dead away on the floor. "U R JUNG" I write under my DORA on the drink napkin. I hold it up at him.

"Have we met?" he says – smiling pretty much like a Cheshire cat.

I shake my head no and smile.

"Let's get it on," the girlboy yells, meaning let's dance, so we do, all four of us move like a single organism out to the pulsing larger organism that is people dancing.

The dude can dance.

I don't mean like a dude his age. I mean like a dancer. Like a real dancer. Like a dancer on stage. He moves like water. He embodies the bass of the music. He looks like desire. He's fucking mesmerizing. His hips do things not even hip-hoppers achieve. He's fast – he's slow – he's barely moving. His shoulders lose their bone structure. And he does this head shoulder chest hips thing that kind of makes you want to take your clothes off really fast. The smell of patchouli and sweat and really great shampoo dizzy me. His hair, it's perfect. He slips his arm around the boygirl he releases he slides his hands onto the girlboy's hips releases he bump-grinds me from behind with his hands locked around my abdomen I rock my head back he slips a pill into my mouth I close my eyes I don't care what it is it is good. Then the girlboy is behind me and up against me and the boygirl is in front of me pressing in until I'm a Dora sandwich and I hope it lasts a really, really long time. I'm creaming my jeans and my nips? Hard as ball bearings. I close my eyes. I feel someone tugging the belt loop of my skinny jeans and I let myself be led by the hip and spun and held close it smells like rain.

Obsidian.

We are more or less entwined, muscular and wet, moving in and out of each other inside sound and light. She is laughing. She throws her head back and her sheet of black hair cuts the air and the obsidian around her neck, I lick it, I suck it, I taste the salt of her. If I could choose when to die, I'd choose this moment, a little death inside the wordless bliss of her body.

Hours later, spent, baptized by sweat, I step outside for a cig.

Attractive older dude is standing with one foot against the building, finishing a joint. He looks over at me, smiles, offers me a toke. I hold my cig up indicating I'm good. He nods and exhales the maryjane way. I light up. Inhale. We both stare at the night sky. Seattle's glow blots out the array of stars, but we both know they are up there. Life is good.

Then a fucking rat walks right in front of us, pauses to look up with its nasty little marble eyes and its shitty-ass rodent tail, and scurries away.

I jump back a bit and my face twists all up. I mean gross.

"Au contraire," Jung says, reading my mind. "Animal totems are primordial symbols of the collective unconscious." He sucks his fatty and holds his breath, then continues. "Think of the Aborigines, the Celts, the Egyptians, Chinese and Native American cultures …" He points the joint down to the ground. "Our friend the rat? The rat totem indicates a pronounced drive for success. An almost uncanny ability to adapt. A cunningness … and the ability to defend oneself aggressively when necessary. Perhaps you need only to adjust your state of mind to see the rat's relation to you."

I point to myself and give him a what-the-fuck look.

Jung laughs. He wets the tip of his joint with his tongue and puts it in his pocket. He puts his hand on my shoulder. "Well, it wasn't there for me, Dora."

And then he walks back into the club. I watch his hair as he walks away.

I stare at the cig in my hand. Smoke curls up toward my face. So the guy is obviously sexually open, has no problem with recreational drugs, loves to dance, and digs animal ju-ju. I take a big-ass drag off my cig, then flick it. It bounces on the pavement and glows for a moment.

I just have one question.

Why the fuck couldn't *this* dude have been my therapist?

19.

"WHAT DO YOU MEAN YOU DON'T KNOW HOW IT HAPPENED?"
I write. I press down super fucking hard with a red Crayola
crayon on a napkin at Shari's, and thrust the napkin pretty much
into Ave Maria's face.

"Well I just mean I didn't think it would do any harm," Ave
Maria goes.

I snatch the little napkin back and break the goddamn
crayon trying to write an answer … I have to get a new napkin
and crayon. The napkins and crayons and straws and silverware
and shit are all at this mini station in the center of Shari's
restaurant. It's exactly like the medicine cabinet deal in the ER.
Maybe the whole world works like this – little substations in life.
I grab a wad of napkins and a black Crayola and some Tabasco
for good measure and go back to the table.

The orange gloom of Shari's feels a little like we're sitting
in a bowl of puke. It's two a.m. so there aren't too many other
customers – a table of goths across the restaurant – jeez did I ever
look that dorkish? A couple of truckers on barstools, a gaggle of
rotund nurses I sincerely hope I've never seen before. Cops don't
congregate until around four a.m.

Obsidian sucks on a banana milkshake and fondles a plate-
ful of bacon. Little Teena downs steak and eggs. Ave Maria
polishes off a plate of pancakes with whip cream and strawber-
ries all over them. She's got whip cream smeared on her chin.
Yes, it's a perfect joke. But I'm in no mood.

"What's the big deal?" Little Teena asks. "It's just a few Facehooker friends and YouTuboners that are looking at it, and no one really knows what they're looking at anyway, right? Plus it's pretty dark. It's not like there was proper lighting. I mean, the troll's even in the shot a couple of times." He whips out a cigarette and a lighter. Lights up.

A waitress waddles over and scowls at him and shakes her jowls. "Sir, you can't do that in here. We're a non-smoking establishment." She points to a sign behind Little Teena's head.

"Ah, fair lady," Little Teena says, "so true." He grabs my black crayon, sticks it in his mouth, and lights it. The waitress backs away like she's a little frightened.

I snatch the black Crayola back, blow the flame out, and rub some of the melted black on my lips. Then I douse it in my glass of water. Smells like melted kid hope.

My head itches. My hair is coming back but I look … patchy. I wipe my mouth with the sleeve of my hoodie – great. I'm so pissed I'm frothing a little. I suck spit back into my mouth and finish what I'm writing and shove the napkin over to Little Teena. "It's not FINISHED. Don't you get it? It's MINE."

"OK, OK," Little Teena says, using the napkin to dab at his forehead.

"I'm sorry I'm sorry I'm sorry," Ave Maria sort of whimpersings at me. "This is the I'm sorry song." She improvises a happy little tune. I look at her. She makes her eyes all big. She rests her head on her fists atop those goddamn pencil-thin wrists. "So soooooooorrrrrrrrrrry," she sings. She pulls the hood of her hoodie up around her head and yanks the strings tight. In a neon pink hoodie with the hood pulled tight around her face, well, it's pretty impossible to be mad at someone who looks like a bright pink singing penis with a girlish face. She blinks.

I write: "your sorry song stinks" and throw it at her.

The problem is this. Ave Maria told one of the teen misfits we let view the footage on the wall next to the troll statue that he could film it on his fucking iPhone. "I guess," she said, out of earshot, so I didn't know it was even happening. Sometimes she just doesn't think.

Well he filmed it all right, but the new G4 iPhones? Yeah. They have H D video recording and FaceTime video calling. So the guy pretty much filmed the whole rough cut and shot it off to god knows how many of his wanker little buddies … there's no way to stop the transmission of images once they signal through the flames. I'm so pissed off I want to punch a hole in the crappy pumpkin-color vinyl booth seats. Ave Maria bobs up and down a little. No way am I gonna laugh. I try for a Stop. Moving. Now. Face. I write: "you've got cum on your chin" and slide another napkin over to Ave Maria.

"Nuh uh!" she says, then wipes, then tastes it, then smiles.

"Anyone want the rest of my bacon?" Obsidian asks, holding a slab of swine up in the air.

I give her the you know I want the bacon, asshole look and she smiles and hands it over. Everyone else gives me what's left of their bacon too. Everyone knows bacon is my favorite food. I chew and stew. The sound of my chewing is all anyone says for a bit. The chorus of short orders and grill sizzling is in the background. I half want to record.

"I was only trying to help," Ave Maria says. "I thought if more people saw it," she stabs a strawberry with her fork and chucks it over my head, "we could get you out of your fucked-up dungeon household and back into the world – I was just trying to create … whadya call it?" She looks pleadingly at Little Teena.

"Buzz," Little Teena says, lighting and smoking his straw. Burned plastic smell.

"Yeah! That. Buzz," Ave Maria says. She shuts up and puts her neon pink head back on top of her wrists. "Don't be hatin' on me, Ida," Ave Maria says. "Or I'll cry. Like right here. In Shari's. Really loud."

I study her face. I think I know what that would sound like, given her high notes. Her eyes well up.

"Goddamn it," I quickly scrawl out on the paper placemat,

"don't fucking cry." My cell vibrates in my hoodie pocket just underneath my rib cut. I don't care who it is. I'm with the only people besides Marlene that matter, so fuck it. It buzzes and buzzes against me. Maybe it'll make my rib cut scab bleed. Whoever you are? Leave a message, punkass. I figure it's Mrs. K. She can suck it.

"Look," Little Teena says all fatherly, "that footage won't last long on Facehooker because they'll figure out there's giant COCK going on sooner than later."

Ave Maria is bobbing her head up and down maniacally. "Yeah," she goes, "you can't have vag or tits or cock on Facehooker."

Little Teena douses his straw in his coffee. "I can figure out a way to hose the signal on YouTube, but it'll take me at least a day. So will you get your panties out of a twist and calm down? By the time you finish your man movie, it will be a goddamn masterpiece. Check that big beautiful ego of yours, madame artiste." He puts me in a faux headlock and nuggies me.

I wrestle free. "Fuck. You." I write, then: "I'm not wearing panties." Then I charley horse him.

"OW. That fucking hurt, you know," Little Teena says. "Good thing I have blubber. I'm a higher mammal."

"What about me," Ave Maria goes, bopping up and down, "don't I get one?" She's smiling like a giddy little penis cartoon.

"You, my bulimic beanpole, have no blubber," Little Teena says.

I give Ave Maria a good kick in the shin underneath the table.

"Thank you!" she sings five octaves higher than human.

Then we're just who we are again. My cell buzzes my gut again. I whip it out of my hoodie pocket. Huh. No idea who that number belongs to. Must be Indians trying to sell me something. That could make decent soundscape though, so I hold my phone to my ear to listen to the voicemail.

"Gross. My thighs are stuck to the seats," Ave Maria says. She's wearing old-school navy-blue gym shorts and white tube socks. Before we get our check, we make a break for it out into the parking lot, a fat waitress with sweat stains from her pits to her boobs chasing us and screaming, "You dirty little fuckers, get your asses back here!" But it's not like she's gonna, you know, catch us, and like I said, the cops don't congregate before 4:00. Obsidian shoots her the bird and takes her T-shirt off and swings it around in the air and throws it in our wake. Briefly I'm stung by the beauty of her undershirt. That Italian white ribbed stretchy kind. Did I think she'd be wearing a bra?

My voicemail kicks in as we run. "I have been trying to reach you. You have something of value that I am in a position to procure. I have a lucrative offer to make to you." I don't even listen to the rest. Must be a wrong number. Doesn't even make any sense. I shove my cell back into my hoodie pocket. Whoever that is can wait.

We run. Together. Chaotic and mismatched. I may not be able to yell, but I can sure as shit run, and nothing beats the sound of Docs on pavement. I flip on my H4n in my Dora purse. Clompclompclompclompclomp. Beautiful. My heart pounding. My rib cut stinging. I still have the crayon. I put the Crayola crayon in my mouth between my teeth. I forgive Ave Maria.

"To the cigarettes!" Little Teena yells, with his arm jammed forward and his lighter lit like we're leading some kind of teen monster charge, a crass ample gay boy, an anorexic pink penis cartoon girl in tube socks, a badass Native American, and a raging mute – I bite therefore I am – through the black Crayola of night.

20.

"YOUR FATHER WOULD LIKE TO SPEAK TO YOU."

That's what I wake up to after maybe two and a half hours of sleep. The voice of Mrs. K. through the crack of my bedroom door. For a second I think I'm dreaming, but nope, I have to pee and my rib cut hurts.

"I know you were not here last night," Mrs. K. says in a low demon tone from the other side of my bedroom door.

Creepola.

"Don't think I won't tell him," Mrs. K. says.

Who does she think she is, anyway? This is my home. Even though I wish it would blow up. But I see the angle. She's staking her territory. Peeing on things and leaving her scent. Rearranging spoons, I bet. Clever twat.

I pull my covers over my head. Ugh. Why do I even come home anymore? I fucking hate this godforsaken place. I live in a Fellini movie. Under the covers, everything looks black and blue. Cool. It's kind of peaceful. I should film under here.

"Now, Ida," the she-vixen goes.

I roll out of bed and into my skinny black jeans. Not sure how many days I can wear this same underwear. Starting to smell a little too much like apples. I rub my head. Feels like ... Astroturf. I check my face in the computer screen. Wow. I guess that's what insomniacs must look like. Like someone spooned out little hollows under their eyes. Cave eyes. Fuck. I don't mind telling you. I am no way looking forward to this. But later today I get to see my Sig. For reasons I can't even begin to explain, it gives me strength. He ain't my grandpa and I sure as shit ain't Heidi, but you got to take what you can get.

I open my bedroom door. I walk down the hall of family. At the end is my parents' bedroom – but that hardly seems like a good thing to call it these days. It's the fucking father room. Where everything that will happen next gets born. As I walk down the hall toward the fucking father room the floor seems to pulse. Ew. It smells like middle age.

Propped up in bed with a gazillion pillows I've never seen before, underneath a bizarro Asian-design comforter my mother would have eaten glass before ever buying, is the man formerly known as Dad. He's clean-shaven. Mrs. K. is standing next to him holding a towel and the safety razor I used to give myself this bitchin' head. She looks so proud of herself. Her lipstick is gleaming. Her eyes give her away though. Here comes Ida's ass-whoopin', I bet she's thinking. Are her tits saluting something?

I don't know how else to say this but to just say it. That clean-shaven guy in the bed? The one with the sunk-in cheeks and knotty throat and silver hair? That's not my dad. I mean it is, it has to be, right? But I don't even recognize him. It's like aliens re-placed my dad with some Frankenstein they cooked up in a spaceship to look human. Um, clearly someone needs to buzz-trim that ear hair, people. He's got an oxygen thingee in his nose. A tank next to his bed. His pajama shirt is unbuttoned and I can see a giant red railroad track going from his sternum down toward his belly button. Open-heart surgery scar. When I look at it I can't feel my legs and my breath jackknifes and I get the spins. I look immediately away from the red railroad track between me and his internal organ and up at the ceiling.

Up on the ceiling? Of fucking course. A dong-shaped crack. Huge. Like a giant dong spying on me. Told you, Fellini movie.

"Ida," my father says. I look not at him, but kinda to the left of his ear. Where did my dad's voice go? This guy sounds like …

like Alan Arkin. No shit. Soft and nasal and a little like he's just hit puberty.

I got no voice, so I just try to look at his ... jesus, when did the color blue leave my father's eyes? Steel-color piss holes. Could the alien theory have merit?

"I've been meaning to speak to you."

I look back up to the ceiling. Then at my own belly. Wonder how long that sentence has been true. Years, I'd wager.

Mrs. K. wipes the razor up and sets it down on the bedside table. She pretends to pull the covers up around this guy in the bed playing the role of my dad. He smiles. Is it true all men just want a series of mothers?

"Look," he says, adjusting himself against all that poofiness, "this is a difficult time."

No. Fucking. Shit. Sherlock. I look at Mrs. K. I look back at the alien.

"I'm going to need you to be a little more adult," the alien says.

Adult. Right. Like you two?

"Until I'm up and about ..."

I shoot a set of eye bullets over at Mrs. K. She's grinning with no teeth. I half expect some mechanical tongue to shoot out and slit my throat. Fuck her for smelling good. That dang Lancôme perfume.

"Please, can I count on you to ... please help Peppina—"

BRAIN STOP. Oh my fucking god. I suck in a breath and hold it. Peppina? Her name is Peppina? What the fuck kind of name is Peppina? I laugh. Luckily nothing comes out sound-wise. All they see is my shoulders sort of spasming. Peppina stops smiling. Pretty sure she's grinding her teeth. I want so badly to go S'up, Peppina Peppilepticpepperonina? right this second. But I can't.

"—as much as possible," he continues. "She is giving of herself quite a lot to be here with me at this time. Ida. Do you understand me?"

Oh, I understand you all right, Daddy. I nod my head slowly up and down. I shove my hands in my jeans pockets. I shrug, and tilt my teen head, giving them the universal 'sthat all? gesture.

"You may go," my father says.

Peppina looks disappointed that I didn't get swatted. Or rolled in butter and set on fire.

I exit the fucking father room. It's right then and there that I decide. I'm not using Vivaldi as the soundtrack in the Sig movie when his wang shoots blood. I'm using the recording of my father breathing from when he was in the hospital. Sometimes fast, sometimes slow. In a loop.

My real father's been abducted by aliens and captured by a strange big-titted demon vixen. My real mother's in Vienna turning more and more beige. Pretty soon she'll be transparent.

Which pretty much makes me an orphan, I figure. My cell vibrates. Well hell. It's that weird number from before. I don't answer. I go into my bedroom. I throw my backpack onto my bed. I pack the SD cards with all the audio and video of my Sig movie. I pack a few new pairs of underwear. I pack my Mantegazza book, my purple Sharpie, Xanax, Vicodin, and Percocet. Two joints. A tiny bit of blow I have left from dosing the Sig. I pack cigarettes, a Pixies T-shirt, my earbuds. I pack my Swiss Army Knife Elite. I check the voicemail on my iPhone. This time I sit on the edge of the bed and listen.

"Hello, Ida. I've been trying to reach you. Through certain … mutual channels, shall we say, it has come to my attention that you have something … well, I'm very much interested in something you have. Some video footage, I believe? Could you perhaps return my call – I can assure you, I can make it very well worth your while."

What the fuck? Pervola? Somebody's dad? A cop? Mutual channels, what the fuck does that mean? I make a pit stop at my computer and do a reverse phone number look up. Odd. What comes up? Hill and Knowlton Inc. Big-time PR agency in

Seattle. Um, they do Microsoft. What the fuck would they want with me? Gotta be a wrong number. A hoax. But I really like the idea of using it for soundscape loops so I hope the dude calls back and calls back.

How does he know my name? Whatevs. Doesn't matter. Life is a Fellini flick. No time.

I don a pair of Steve McQueen mirror shades. I put on a black leather biker jacket. Quick search of the pockets reveals more Vicodin and hey! A barely touched box of Hot Tamales. Ave Maria will cream. On my way outta the hellhole, I see Mrs. K.'s purse. I nab her wallet and take all her cash and a couple of her credit cards. Christ. She's got pictures of the midget demons in her wallet. Could there be two uglier children? Spawn gone wrong, that's for sure. Are their ears pointed? Then I spot something else on the kitchen counter – pearl drop earrings – undoubtedly Mrs. K.'s, double undoubtedly a gift from the alien formerly my father. I snatch 'em up and put them in my mouth like sugar cubes and flee. *I'm sucking on the pearl drops, Siggy*. Smile.

Luckily, I have a shrink.

21.

ON THE BUS FROM CAPITOL HILL DOWN TO PIKE I LOOK
around at my fellow mobile inmates. Why is it that people on
buses look like tired sacks of shit? Literally – like someone shat
sacks of us onto these ass-shaped plastic seats that smell like
rank old monkey balls. No one on a bus looks cool. And you can
bet your bottom dollar that there is always a whack job just
waiting for his perfect moment to go bus fuck mental. Don't even
get me started on the fat-assery of the drivers. You know they got
a Pabst hidden down by the gears somewhere. Christ. Last year
some middle-aged gasbag driver actually ran over two people
and dragged them half a block before noticing. Everyone on the
bus screaming their heads off for her to stop.

I'm sweating the sweat of not knowing what to expect. I'm
on my way to see Sig. I'm all fucked up. I can't talk, I'm homeless, I'm an orphan, I need to change my underwear. What am I
gonna do when I get there, write him notes for an hour? Do a tap
dance? Strip naked and masturbate?

Hell, maybe he's got cops there waiting for me. It's a
possibility.

I look out the shitty window at the passing city crap. Then
I have a pop-up thought: I wonder if Marlene would let me crash
with her for awhile?

Marlene works at Sea-Tac Airport as a security officer three
days a week. She, well, OK, "he," since we're talking about her
man job, works at one of the full-body X-ray huts. You know, the

ones for international flight folks where you have to stick a chunk of lead in your pants if you don't want them to see your junk.

When he's a she, she sings Eleanora Fagan songs at a tranny jazz club cabaret on the south edge of Capitol Hill. Holy shit does Marlene have some pipes. In her voice Eleanora Fagan comes back from the dead. You haven't lived until you've heard Marlene sing "What Is This Thing Called Love" or "Summertime." In fact, I've got her on the Zoom H4n right now. In my Dora purse. "God Bless the Child." I ease up the volume. I feel slightly less deranged.

Poor Eleanora Fagan though. Marlene told me all about her. You know Billie Holiday died in a hospital room where police were waiting to take her to jail? Fucking typical. Cirrhosis of the liver and drug addiction is what it said on her death certificate. What it should have said is that her life was the suck. The only beautiful thing about it lived in her throatsong.

The bus is pointed straight downhill. Always makes me feel like I'm gonna get a nosebleed. The guy across from me has a soiled crotch and a ski parka the color of puke. He's wearing a hair nest. The woman two seats up has a big weird mole right in the center of the back of her head poking through what's passing for her hair. Then there's a DING and we stop and some whitey middle-aged corporate dude with a Dolce and Gabbana black leather man shoulder purse gets on. Is he fucking lost? Yeah. Where YOU gonna sit, Mr. Corporate Shiny Pants? Oh. Nice. He's wearing sunglasses. He sits directly in front of me. Blocking my view of mole head. His hair has a weird silver sheen to it and smells like … important flowers.

I reach into my Dora and pump the playback of Marlene singing "Strange Fruit" – low enough that people look up a bit, but not enough for them to figure out it's coming from the lump that is me. Marlene's voice calms me a little. Scent of magnolias sweet and fresh. Then the sudden smell of burning flesh. It's the kind of voice you wish would sing you to sleep at night. I rock in my seat. Sure, a little autistic. But who cares?

Fancy man figures out where the voice is coming from and turns around so his sunglasses are looking at me. Can you imagine? The nerve. I pick the hell out of my nose for no reason. Big drill. Wipe it on the window. Yeah that's right, turn the fuck back around, guy made of reflective surfaces. We bus mutants way outnumber you.

Then it hits me. I've seen this dude before. In the restaurant. With Sig. The day I recorded the exchange where Sig fainted. Right after this dude told him he was going big time – the show –

television megastardom. The guy who said, and I quote, "we need your teen monster girl." Why didn't I see his ferret ass before?

Silverhead turns back around and leans over till he's nearly in my lap. "Hello, Ida," slickster says, taking off his man shades, "I've been trying to reach you."

Thoughts roll around in my noggin like dice in a cup. The phone messages? This guy? But why? Ew. I shoot a desperate glance out the bus window – at the bottom of the hill is my stop, my Sig, my escape. Thirty seconds tops. I pick my nose some more and laugh like I'm high on THE DOPE and make chimp faces at him. Most people are scared shitless of out of control teens.

He's unfazed. He stands up like he's gonna come sit with me. Gross. He's wearing black leather gloves. In no situation is a man wearing black leather gloves a good thing.

I stand up too and do an improv chimp dance in the aisle. Chimps can be deadly, remember.

"Please take your seat," the Pabst bus driver says over some shitty bus mic, but really all we hear is static: "peeeezzzzz-zshhtaaaaakeshrrrrrummmfrah."

My upper lip sweats. My rib cut stings. My head itches. Cartoons from my bullshit childhood populate my skull. Stranger danger! Stranger danger! OK homeboy, I got about thirty seconds till my stop. You got something for me? Bring it. I take a defensive posture – kind of a mix between Bruce Lee and Harry Potter. My hands in menacing shapes. Savage chimp grimace.

"My dear girl, there's no reason for alarm," silverslick says, putting his hands out like to the sides either like a rich well-dressed Jesus or like he's gonna grab me, but the bus is jostling too much and the bus driver is yelling "Sssssshiiiiiiiitooowww-wwnpeeeeessssshhhzzz" and the hill we're barreling down makes it so we're all just this side of falling and—

DING.

I'm a girl gone.

22.

HONESTLY, I'VE NEVER BEEN MORE GLAD TO SEE SOME-
one I just fucked over royal in all my life.

When I get up the elevator to Sig's office the door is already
open so I tumble in. I'm out of breath from running. The way
we're standing there – it feels like we are in a movie. Zoom in. I
look at Sig. Sig looks at me. Fuck. I whip out my cell from my
Dora purse. I quickly text: *lost my fkg voice. weird guy chsed me
off bus.* His pants buzz. He pulls his cell out of his pocket and
reads.

"I see," Sig says, "let's just calm down a minute, shall we?
Come sit down." He guides me to the couch and then closes the
door to the office.

I sit on the dreaded black leather couch to catch my breath,
the pad of paper and Sharpie in my hand. Sig sits in the camel-
back chair. He crosses his legs. He pulls a cigar out from his pocket.
A silver lighter. We sit and stare at each other. It's awkward.
Bordering on creepola. He looks like he's waiting for something.
A whole fucking minute of silence passes. Is he waiting for me?
I'm so far beyond an anxiety attack I could power a bus. Fuck it.
I make an executive decision. I jam my hand into my skinny
jeans pocket and pop a Xanax. I madly chew it like baby aspirin.
Sig doesn't move or comment. I close my eyes. I hold my breath
for seven seconds. I blow out for seven seconds. I do it seven
times. Sig doesn't move or comment. When I open my eyes, he's
still waiting. For me.

OK. I can breathe again. I guess maybe that's fair. It's my move. I look down at my pad of paper. My ears are hot. I text, *you hate me, rt?* He reads his phone and I look at the ceiling. Covered with genitalia cracks. Of course.

He studies my words. Christ dude, it's four fucking words. Finally he says, "Have you ever seen a character on TV called Jung?"

I stare at him. I blink the big-eyed blink of an idiot. Then try to stop. What the fuck? He lights his cigar. The air between us is suddenly heavy with a deep tobacco musk. For reasons I can't explain I think of Heidi. I'll give him this, he's a smoothie.

Turns out, I have seen this Jung character on TV. He's a teleshrink. Mostly his gig is about dreams and animals and new-age ju-ju-whammy. But his show is huge.

Yes, I text, *he's rich*. Where exactly are we going with this? It's amazing how fast the smell of a cigar goes from aromatic to gag me.

He reads. "Ah, then you are, as usual, ahead of the game," Sig says.

How is this helping again? Hello? Voiceless chick sitting across from you? Recently chased off of a bus by some chester the molester? Sig smokes. The smoke, well this is going to sound weird but the smoke seems to be in his control. It wafts up in great curls toward the ceiling, then falls a little above my head, like it's turned to look at me, to study me, to record my actions and behaviors. Man. I must be in pretty bad shape.

Sig stands up and glides by me on his way to his bookshelf. I have to twist around so I can see him. He does that pet the books thing. Great. Maybe I was wrong to come here. I accidentally stare at his wang area. Flat as a pancake. Get a grip.

From the bookshelf where he's stroking his collection, Sig says, "Jung is a hack. Former colleague of mine. Former student, actually. Unfortunately for me, he has come back into my life with very … serious repercussions."

Now I'm pissed. I punch my little iPhone letters with venom. *Wtf dz this hv 2 do w me?* I consider chucking my iPhone at him.

He reads. "Everything, my dear Ida," he says.

Okeydokey. My shrink's toppled his dreidel. And it's probably partly my fault. Karma's a bitch, right? I'm fucked. I stand up and rub my almost-hair and make like I'm gonna leave. What was I even thinking? But when I get near him he gently grabs my arm.

"Ida," he says, "please. Sit." He pats my shoulders. He guides me back to the couch. "All will be revealed." He smiles. Briefly he doesn't look insane.

I open my mouth. I try to talk. A sad little breath-rasp comes out. I sit down on the couch. More and more with my little gimpy iPhone I feel like that chick in the chick flick *The Piano*. But it's all I've got. *Look,* I text. *My dad had a huge coronary. My mum fled 2 vienna. Stuk w my dads ho n demon midgets. Hav no voic. Sum perv trid 2 grab me. Things aren't ql, ok?*

He reads.

He nods.

He chuckles.

Yuck it up, asshole. He looks up without saying a goddamn word.

Fine. Well, let's just wrap this little charade up then. I text, *Dy hv any blo? Top drawer of desk? Coz so far dats d only thing here to help. Jst lite me up and il b outa yr hair.* I sit with my hands at rest. Without drama.

The dude remains unflappable. Dang. I actually sort of admire it.

"I do, as you suggest, have benzoylmethylecgonine. But I think we've both partaken adequately. No?" He leans toward me. "Do not despair, beautiful Ida. I can help you. But in order for me to help you," he puts his hand on his own throat, "you will have to help me."

Jesus. I shoulda known. Does it all really come down to

this? Am I gonna have to blow my shrink? Pass out? Wake up in the emergency room? Would that make us even?

He laughs. Like he knows what I'm thinking. "It isn't that," he reassures me. "And besides, you already gave me, shall we say, a colossal rise on that score?"

Well I'll be goddamned. He certainly seems to be taking that well.

"I'll get straight to the point," he says, leaning in even closer, and now his eyes look like two silver dimes. "There is a certain video in your possession."

My neck bristles and I shoot my knees together, making a clunk sound.

"Oh, come now. Don't look so surprised. I know because my publicist knows, and he knows because his minions found it on … what do you call it? YouTube? Aptly named for a nation of egocentric children." He turns and walks over to my clock present on his desk. Yep, the one with the camera in it. He bends over so his face is directly in front of it. He smiles and waves. "Hello," he says into its face. Then he blows cigar smoke at it.

Busted.

I look down into my lap. I have to pee. My knees itch. When he speaks again his voice is a father's voice. Not my father's voice, but the voice some other father would use if he was angry or stern. I'm no idiot. I know what a father voice is supposed to sound like.

Gotta up it a notch. I text, *IK bout yr sho*.

Sig reads, then itches his head. Then itches it harder. Then coughs.

"Ida, I need that video. I cannot let it fall into the wrong hands. There are people who want it. They want to profit from it. They … well. Let me show you." He paces back and forth. He coughs. Then he walks over to his desk drawer and I think maybe he's going to bring us on over some blow after all but instead he hits the playback on his desk phone. Voice message.

"Sigmund – look. What people want these days isn't reality TV. They want beyond reality TV. They want the next level. They're hungry for it. Hell, they'd kill for it. What happened to you – it's the next level. No one has ever seen anything like it – uncut, uncensored. HBO baby. HBO wants the Emergency Room scene. Your ER drama blows those fake TV ER dramas out of the water."

"That," Sig explains, "was the man who chased you. He wants to offer you a hefty sum of money for that footage, Ida. He wants it for the big show he's made of my life's work."

Sig stands up and walks over to his bookshelf again. He runs his palm over an entire row of shit-brown bound books. Like a hundred of 'em all in a row. "These are my case studies. My life's work. The labor of my body, my mind, my very soul. This one," he puts his hand on a slim volume at the very end of the row, "is yours. I named you 'Dora.' This is your story."

U named me after my purse? I text.

"No, Ida. I named you after my niece. A girl of your age who was both cruel, and once, kind to an old man." He runs his hands back across the spines of his case studies. "Really, they are all that's left of me." He looks at the ground.

Jeez, is he gonna cry? For a second I feel sorry for him.

"They want to make my books into televised excrement! It seems there is very little I can do to stop them. They even want ... Jung. My ungrateful nemesis. To play me." He drops his head. He walks back over to his camel-back chair and sits down. His shoulders look smaller. He smokes his cigar. It smells briefly like benevolent grandfathers.

We sit in silence staring at each other. My breathing is sort of funny. I hold my breath in an attempt to straighten it out. Don't be a pussy. Stay frosty.

"Seeing as you are responsible for this video coming about," he says through his cigar smoke, "I feel it is my prerogative to ask that you give it to me, and only to me. I think," he puts his cigar in an ashtray on the table between us, "you owe me that.

It's a matter of ethics." I stare at the stub of cigar. Yep, looks like a brown, pudgy little dick. Erectionless. Why am I here?

I study him through the smoke dissipating between us. He's right, of course, what I did to him on one level does suck giant dong, but it's MY art. I made it. It's what I do. Hell, it's the only thing I know how to do. I get to decide what to do with it. Goddamn it. My art is all I am. I don't say anything. I don't move. I try to look at him like I'm the Statue of fucking Liberty. Concrete. Like I can pee standing up.

So he gets to be the ethical one and I have to surrender my art? Fuck that noise. I put my phone down. This calls for a more careful approach. I open my Dora the Explorer purse. I pull out my beloved purple Sharpie. I scan the room for paper. I see a pad of paper on his desk, nab it, and scrawl out: "What's n it for me?" I hold the pad up for him to read. Then I fake-smoke my Sharpie. Smells like felt pen.

He smiles. "If you agree to give the video to me, Ida, I will help you not only to recover your voice, but I will help to release you from your current situation. For good. Forever."

Sly bastard. I don't know what he means by that but he's for goddamned sure got something up his sleeve. I nod my head up once at him in the universal street lingo of s'up.

Then he drops the bomb. "Ida, I've arranged for a scholar-ship to attend Tisch School of the Arts at New York University. Free. It's one of the finest film institutes in the country. Where you can, my lovely, raging girl, make any films you like."

Motherfucker. Wonder how long the sly dog has been sitting on that one.

You know what I look like right this second? A kid with a pink plastic purse who is smoking a Sharpie like a candy cigarette. If my knees were skinned I'd be about, oh, eight years old. I take the goddamn Sharpie out of my mouth. My mouth hangs open. I don't know how to do this I don't know how to dot hisIdon'tknowhowtodothisFUCK. Even inside my voiceless girl sack, I'm speechless.

I'm baffled, but I'm not dead. I text therefore I am. *Wl think bout it*, I text, even though it makes me feel like someone I don't know.

23.

I WISH I COULD SAY LIFE GIVES YOU A SUCKER SHOT once in awhile, but my empirical data has shown that it's nearly always a one-two punch.

Before I can even come to from the stun of what Sig just said to me, I find Ave Maria and Little Teena sitting on the kerb outside his office. Little Teena stands up. Ave Maria bounces like a pinball.

"They've got Obsidian!" Ave Maria squeals, cupping her elbows.

My eyes go big. I put my head in the direction of Little Teena.

"What she means is, Obsidian's been arrested."

My breathing immediately clusterfucks and my head fills with cotton. I see stars. Do NOT faint. Hold it together you pussy. I close my eyes and picture a tree with roots. I try to feel my feet like roots in the ground. I have no fucking idea where that came from but I have a million mile away flint of memory that my mother told me that when I was eight. Then again, I'm prone to hallucination. I kick one foot with the other to try to keep from going numb.

I grab Little Teena's shoulders and put my head down some and give him the sternest look I can muster.

"OK, listen," he says. "Try to stay calm. Obsidian was up at the rez near Coeur d'Alene to see her cousin and her dad's brother came at her. Drunk, I guess. Pinned her to the ground and started trying to … you know. The cousin jumped on his back to try and stop him and Obsidian, well, Obsidian …"

I don't need to know what the next sentence is. I know. Obsidian took her shard of obsidian that hangs from her neck and cut him.

"She cut him. Across the neck. Almost his jugular. Fucker nearly bled out right there."

"Like in the movies!" Ave Maria sings.

I give her a drop-dead look.

"Or not," she whimpers.

I drop to the kerb like childhood leaving a body. I put my head between my legs. Don't pass out. Don't pass out. Don't motherfucking pass out. Your feet are roots in the ground your feet are roots in the ground I can't feel my feet.

"Ida!" An Ave Maria high note.

Then Little Teena's hand on my back.

In my head there are so many things I don't understand. Songs, words, images I don't even know where they came from. Are they from my life, or did I dream them up? Is there a difference? I open my eyes and sit up. It's dusk. The clouds streaking through the sunset make the sun look wrinkled. Maybe it doesn't matter what's real and what you dream up. Maybe what you dream up keeps you alive. I can feel Little Teena rubbing my back. I can hear Ave Maria humming. I look at the wrinkled-up sun again. The sun in the Seattle sky is a girl belly button above low-waist skinny jeans.

I stand up. I retrieve my iPhone from my Dora purse. I text, *Whrs she. Xactly.*

Little Teena and Ave Maria's asses buzz. They check their cells simultaneously. God, I love technology.

Ave Maria says, "They've got her in a juvie center near Renton!"

I text, *Juvie? She's nearly 18. Whyd thy snd her 2 juvie?*

Little Teena touches my shoulder as gently as a loving

brother ever could. "Ida, Obsidian's not nearly eighteen, honey. Obsidian turns sixteen next month. Didn't you know?"

See what I mean? One-two punch. Only this isn't about me. This is about the girl I love. With all my heart. I love a girl named Obsidian and somebody's gotta save her from girlhood before it's too late. This time my feet aren't just on the ground. They're in the ground. I'm a motherfucking girl tree. I text, *'Cum on. we're goin.'*

"Going where?" Ave Maria peeps, running alongside me with her hands and arms inexplicably windmilling.

'GunA gt my hom gal outa thr,' I text.

Without blinking, or talking, or thinking, Ave Maria pulls on her hair on both sides of her head and sings up toward the falling wrinkled sun, "We're gonna need the Jag," absolutely knowing what it'll mean. Way.

24.

WHILE AVE MARIA AND LITTLE TEENA WORK ON STEAL-
ing the Jag yet again, I stomp my way into night toward Marlene's.
Watching my own Docs on Seattle pavement I have another
epiphany. I don't need home. A daddy. I don't need my mommy.
What I need is my Marlene.

At Sea-Tac Airport Marlene is a he: Hakizamana Ojo. Like
I told you before, Hakizamana Ojo is in charge of manning one
of those full-body scanners. He has a high level of clearance when
it comes to security. He is very good at his job. He's been
promoted three times – even Homeland Security couldn't find
anything weird about him, despite his name. There's probably
no one at Sea-Tac who knows more about security than Hakizamana Ojo. Nor more about genitalia. Nor more about identity
swapping.

One night when Marlene got dumped by some asshat with
a pencil mustache – no doubt one of those hipsters from Portland – we sat on the top of her apartment building and cried and
drank Pabst Blue Ribbon beers. We made a silver and blue beer
can pyramid with the empties. It was pretty big pyramid.
Marlene was crying. A lot. I had no idea what to say or do so I just
sat there like a lump. But a loyal lump.

Finally Marlene said, "When I was a boy in Rwanda my
German father beat my mother within an inch of her life. He beat
her because she'd been raped. Then he left forever. I nursed
my mother back to health. I wore woman clothes. Her clothes. I

wanted to be soft and good like nurses and mothers are. The next month I wore a dress into the township and four boys older than I shoved a truncheon into my anus and beat me within an inch of my life. I managed to make it back home, and my mother had a plane ticket for me. To go to live with my father in Germany. She said, 'You and I are Tutsi. They are killing us everywhere.' She said, 'You will die here if you stay. Take that dress off.' I loved my mother more than anything in the world. By that time she'd been repeatedly raped and had a scar from being burned across one eye. I remember thinking, is that the worst thing that can happen to a person? Death?"

Then Marlene stopped crying. The moon was big. Her rooftop looked lit up like a stage briefly. "I have the ability to make any passport. I can be anyone I like. Forever. Or make anyone into anyone else," she said. Or he. Nothing bad that ever happens to me is going to be as bad as what happened to Marlene. And yet there we were sitting on her rooftop with a PBR pyramid. Just two people with gender issues. I never forgot that moment. How Marlene and Hakizamana were both there. Interchangeable. If need be. In moments of danger or love. We walked back into her apartment leaving the Pabst pyramid as testament to something.

When I arrive at Marlene's, three things are true.

Thing one: Marlene's door is already open.

Thing two: silver slickster bus perv is sitting at her kitchen table drinking a glass of Kirsch.

Thing three: Marlene is pretty much dressed exactly like Barbara Stanwyck in *Double Indemnity*. Pencil skirt, white silk blouse, seamed stockings, killer heels. I mean if Barbara Stanwyck was African-American? Spitting image. I almost laugh.

They look at me. I look at them.

Marlene says, "Ah, Ida. This man says he knows you. I told him I did not think so, but he says that you recently spoke?"

I shake my head no. You have to be ready to be anyone in moments of danger or love.

"Yes, I told him that was rather impossible," Marlene says, standing and walking to the fridge.

"But we do know each other, don't we, Ida?" Pervola says.

There's not much else to do but go ahead and walk in. I do. I sit down at the table. I look at the ceiling. Marlene's rummaging around in the freezer. No, she's chipping ice with an ice pick into a bowl. She comes back with a glass of Kirsch for me. With ice. She smiles.

"Ida, I'd like to make you an offer," slickster says, then turns to Marlene, "perhaps you could help us communicate?"

"Certainly," Marlene says. Under the kitchen table she puts her toe on my toe and gently presses down.

I shoot her a this guy's a dillweed look. She looks down and under the cover of those mega eyelashes and slips me a yes he most certainly is look.

"I'm sorry I alarmed you on the bus," he begins. "That was not my intent."

I clench my ass cheeks. Marlene pushes down again on my toe.

"Look. No sense in pussy-footing around. I'll come straight to the point," he continues. "I'll give you $5,000 for your video footage of Freud. Cash. No strings attached." His smile is smug. He sips his wine.

I watch his lip curl over the lip of the glass. Middle-aged people's mouths are kind of creepy – you can see too much gum. And no one is successful at covering up bad breath.

In my head I go *five grand*? That's like getting a birthday card from Grandma. Five grand doesn't get you shit these days. I tilt my head to the side, raise my hand up in a little fist with a thumb pointing up and pump it in the air at him.

He blanches. Then recovers. "Did I say five grand? I meant twenty-five." He smug-smiles.

Not even close, asshat. I shake my head. I pull out a cig and light it. He eyeballs me. He looks like he's thinking something along the lines of you little shit.

"I see," he says. "Perhaps you have a number in mind?"

I retrieve a Sharpie from my backpack. Slowly and deliberately I write a number on Marlene's kitchen table. $500,000.00. I huff my Sharpie once for punctuation.

That seems to do the trick. His face beets.

His breathing through his nose is quick and hard. It looks like he has to will his mouth to say, "That. Can. Be. Arranged." Teeth clenched.

I look at Marlene. I don't know what she sees in my eyes but what I'm holding in those sockets like little messed-up girl marbles is what the fuck is it with all the money? First Sig's offer, now this? Did I go to sleep and wake up in money land? Is this what being an adult comes down to? You have to speak capital to break your cherry?

Marlene studies my face. Maybe she's studying more than that. We've known each other since I was fourteen. Fourteen, fifteen, sixteen, seventeen, lemme tell you. Those are big years. Everybody always thinks of it as a time of adolescence – just getting through to the real part of your life – but it's more than that.

Sometimes your whole life happens in those years, and the rest of your life it's just the same story playing out with different characters. I could die tomorrow and have lived the main ups and downs of life. Pain. Loss. Love. And what you all so fondly refer to as wisdom. Wanna know the difference between adult wisdom and young adult wisdom? You have the ability to look back at your past and interpret it. I have the ability to look at my present and live it with my whole body. Wanna know what we have in common? Dead dreams. Trust me when I say no adult likes to talk about that.

Plus how do you even know you adult humans have the right interpretations of your own lives? People are like books and movies. There are about a gazillion different interpretations. Deal with it.

I look at Marlene's perfectly coifed blond 1940s wig sitting so artfully on her head. Man that woman slays me.

"That is quite a lot of money," Marlene says, then pulls a cigarette and lighter from her bra, lights the cigarette, and blows out the slowest coolest curl of white smoke – like you only see in black and white flicks. She turns to creepy dude. She blows a bit of smoke right at him and says, "Tell me, what business do you have with a girl who is, what is it," she sizes him up like beef, "a quarter of your age?"

I love Marlene.

I love Marlene.

I love Marlene.

I reach down and into my Dora purse under the table and turn my H4n on.

"One must be careful," she continues, "in this day and age."

Silverfuck pulls out some paperwork from the breast pocket of his suitcoat and lays it out on the kitchen table like it means something.

"I've got a contract here. This is a real deal. I don't have time to bullshit about children. My offer is on the table. I'm only making this offer once though." He then pulls out a silver flask – man what is with all the silver with this guy? And drinks. It's whiskey. I can smell it. I can also smell his godforsaken lunch. Shrimp of some sort. Ew. He holds the flask out toward me. "Ida? What do you say? You ready to make the choice of your life?"

I take the flask. I'm seventeen; I'm not an idiot. I drink his nasty shrimp whiskey. A lot. Most of it. Then all of it. I set the empty flask back down on the table. I shake my head no. That's when the asshole grabs my wrist and twists it and says, "Look you little teen monster bitch, you're gonna hand over that footage or I'm gonna come take it from you. By any means necessary."

Everything next is sound.

The sound of Marlene shoving her chair back and standing up. The sound of silverfuck doing the same. Still holding my wrist so I'm yanked up like a scary doll. The sound of "Get your motherfucking hands off of the girl" coming from Hakizamana Ojo. Deep and true and macho ghetto menacing. The sound of silverfuck saying, "You don't know who you are messing with, faggot."

And then a single, mindbogglingly cool continuous shot: Marlene pulling an ice pick from inside the sleeve of her white silk blouse and crossing over to silverfuck and headlocking him and bending his free arm behind his back and jamming the ice pick up against his neck just enough to make him yell and let go of my wrist.

Told you he was good at his security job.

I back away from the scene. Panting. But not fainting. Sometimes saviors look different than you thought they would.

I wish I could say something really great happened here. But life isn't like it is in the movies. Silverfuck, even in his distorted head and arm lock, begins to laugh. Marlene's eyes go bigger. I look behind me.

Silverfuck narrates. "I hope you don't mind, Ida," he gurgles under the thick choke hold of Marlene, "I've taken the liberty of calling your parents."

In the doorway are Peppina and my ashen alien father. In my gut is the inescapable truth of my life.

"What on earth?" my father says.

"Ida!" she-vixen shrieks.

Only one thing to do. I puke.

25.

IN THE DREAM, I WALK AROUND IN SOME CITY I DON'T know. Classical piano music score. I see cobblestone streets and town squares, which are strange to me except from shitty-ass historical drama flicks. Then I come into a house where I live and find a letter from my mother saying "your father is dead and if you like you can cum." I go down a road and ask about a gazillion times: "where is the station?" But the people are like zombies how they are in dreams. I see a thick wood before me and see the station in front of me and I run toward it, but it's pretty much like running in Jell-O, and I can't reach it.

I wake up. I'm totally sweating. I look over at my digital clock. It's five a.m. And something else. I am drenched between my legs.

The whole rest of the "night" I think about that fucking dream. I know exactly what the Sig would say. He'd say I want my dad dead for betraying me. But I have guilt about that, because, you know, wanting your dad dead is kind of not cool. I know what Siggy would say about the woods, too. He'd say it's a sexual landscape. He'd say what I really want is for Mr. Lechbo K. to penetrate those woods and fuck me silly as revenge against my dumb dad.

Honestly I don't know what crack pipe that guy smokes sometimes.

Wanna know what I think it means?

I think I dream my dad out of the way so I can find a woman.

Maybe my mother. No, I don't forgive her for her lame-ass lapsed motherhood. But I can still hear the sound of her playing piano in my head. I think when she played the piano she was trying to tell me something. Something about art. But then her marriage tanked and she went numbimbo and I turned into me.

I think the woods in the dream are in the way, and yeah, they may be a vag map, but I think I'm supposed to go straight through them – vag to vag – to see for myself what's on the other side. I think she's been keeping a secret all these years.

I put my hand between my legs. Sticky. I bring my hand to my mouth. Salty apples. I roll over on my side. I pull the covers over me. I get fetal. I roll around in the bed under the covers. You come from salty goo. Salty goo comes out of you. Maybe it all boils down to vags, but that's not nothing. Under the covers it's beautiful and dark.

At about eight thirty a.m. I get a knock on my bedroom door. "Ida?" Fucking Peppina the ho. "Are you decent?" she says.

Am I?

After I pull on my skinny jeans and a Velvet Underground T-shirt I open the door. The look on her face is a cross between frightened and fascist. Honest.

She comes in.

She sits on the edge of my bed. If you've lived through teenager you've witnessed several of these sit-downs. They are never, ever, good.

Peppina is wearing a red sweater with a V-neck so low her cleavage looks cavernous. If I was a man there would be no way to talk to this woman and look her in the eye. Hell, even as me I can't look her in the eye. I literally feel vertigo. Like I'm gonna fall into that boob cavern. What a way to go, huh?

"Ida," Peppina says, and briefly I think wow. We have the two stupidest names in the history of the planet. What's so hard about coming up with cool girl names? Like Obsidian.

"Your father thinks perhaps you and I might be able to talk

more easily about things," Peppina says. "Woman to woman." She takes a deep breath.

Dudette. You are so not my mother.

She takes an even deeper breath. I watch her cleavage. Watch out! Those bad boys may blow! I catch myself thinking. Then, really? My idiotic alien dad thinks you should talk things out with me? Perfect.

"I know you are going through a difficult time," she says, "and I want you to know that I understand. I do. My own parents were divorced when I was just ten years old. I want you to know that you can talk to me. Because of that. Because I understand."

If I had a voice right now? I'd tell her to fuck the fuck off. Since I don't? I pick my nose.

She smiles. "Oh Ida. That kind of thing isn't going to work on me. I'm not … stupid."

She scoots over closer to me. I can smell her hoodoo perfume. What's she up to? I sit in my cone of silence and try to will her sweater to fly off.

"Listen," she says in the voice of a vixen, "how about you and I start over? I'd like to take you shopping."

Shopping?

Is this woman insane?

She inches over ever closer and puts her hand on my knee. My crotch goes warm. My face gets hot. I shake my head no.

"Ida," she says, and now she reaches over and holds my face in her hands, "I think we could be friends."

I yank my face away.

Peppina moves so close to me she's nearly sitting on me. She takes my face in her hands again. This time, she holds my jaw more firmly. "Ida, I have strong feelings for you. Why, I remember when you were just a child …"

You are so so not my mother.

I avoid eye contact. I stare down. But you know what's down there. The cavern. Those enormous pendulous orbs.

Whiter than bread. The wicked perfume. Her tits rise and fall with her breathing. The perfume gets all up in my nose. I can't help it. I want to bury my face in her tits. I want to almost maul her like a chimp. Then she lifts my face up toward hers and kisses me about a centimeter away from my lips, all slow motion-y, my mug still between her hands.

I've still got the booger from before, you know.

You know how sometimes you do shit you don't really know where it came from? Yeah. I grab her headful of redhead. My hands sort of disappear in all those waves of auburn hanging around her face and shoulders – I mean it's mythic – I carefully plant the booger in her perfect hair and then? Eye to eye I lay a big hard wet one right on her mouth.

With tongue.

She pulls back. Slaps me a hot one. I smile. The lingering taste of salt and apples … at least to me.

"That was entirely inappropriate," Peppina says, her slap hand on her heaving bosom. Such a harsh voice for a vixen.

"I'm going to speak to your father," she says as she lurches up and toward the door, "your … problems are worse than even I understood."

Exit a vixen, stage left. I gotta confess. As she's walking out my teen door? I watch her ass make its beautiful up and down flex with each step beneath her … what do you even call black pants like that? Vixen slacks? I'm pretty sure I can see wetness in the dark space under her ass and between her legs.

Let's make that shopping date, sister, I go.

In my head I mean.

The second my dad's ho is gone? I shove my bed against my bedroom door. I shove my dresser across the room and dump it onto the bed for weight. I unplug my TV and put that on the bed too. Then I dismantle all the floor-to-ceiling two by fours from my homemade studio and jam the two by fours between the bed and the walls. I step back. Vaguely the whole shebang looks like a spaceship. Also I superglue the doorframe in the knob area. I figure I've got twenty-four hours tops.

To make this room into something they'll never forget.

26.

ON THE WALL OF MY BEDROOM, WITH MY PURPLE SHARPIE
I write "Aphonia." I draw a big bald girl head with an open mouth
around it. I give her very long luxurious eyelashes.

Aphonia literally means "no voice." The Sig taught me that.

On the other side of my bedroom door the bamorama has
begun. It's them. The first round of parental pounding on my
door. The first round of "Ida? Open this door, please." The first
round of my father the alien and his ho-bag redhead. "Ida, you're
going to have to open this door. Ida, this is not appropriate."
The next "Ida" I hear? I chuck my digital clock at the door. As it
flies in the air I see 9:31 p.m. tumbling in space. The thunk stuns
them for a minute. I hear them muttering gibberish in whispers
on the other side of the wood. Then someone tries the doorknob.
Rattlerattlerattle. SUPERGLUE.

My ass buzzes. Whoever it is can suck it.

If you google Aphonia and check out the Wikipedia page
you'll see all this crap about how when a person with Aphonia
prepares to speak, the vocal folds, which ordinarily come
together and vibrate, don't meet. Yeah vocal cord banging is how
talking happens. With Aphonia, there's no banging. So you
are soundless. Aphonia can be caused by injury, but also by fear
or trauma or stress. What I'm saying is, you could, you know, go
voiceless from just being fucked up. Like me.

I retrieve my Zoom H4n from my Dora purse. I put it near
the door and turn it on. It's definitely sound I want. Their idiotic

door poundings. After tonight I'm never going to have to listen to them again.

I rummage around in my Dora purse for my Swiss Army Knife Elite. There's some crumpled-up paper in there. I un-crumple it. Ah. Failed test from school. At school they make us memorize the capitals and main domestic products and political systems of Iceland, of Yugoslavia, of Rwanda. They give us tests with maps that are only the black and white outlines and borders of so-called countries. We're supposed to fill in the names. Write down the data. In the place where Rwanda is I wrote "Marlene" in red. That's the only word I wrote. I failed most of my tests. Tests are for pussies.

I lean on the wall I'm writing on. I think about Obsidian incarcerated in some lock-down halfway house for teen fuck-ups. I think about me barricaded in my room. What we need is a break out. Out of our lives, out of Seattle, out of the dumb script of girl. I draw an outline of a girl on my wall. I give her straight swaths of deep purple hair. And a little necklace with a sharp shard dangling from it. I write "Cuntry."

Ass buzz. Fuck off.

Boom boom boom and Ida Ida Ida at the door. Ida this and Ida that. I grab my Mac mouse and hurl it as hard as I can at the door. For a second I feel bad for it and think I hear a little yelp. But no, it's just Peppeleptic making woman noises.

I wonder where voice lives in a body. Is it in the throat, where the flaps pound each other to death, making us think we've got important fucking things to say? Or is it in the mind, where thoughts crash crazily into each other pinball-y and dinging, until they slide down the chute and out the hole and into the world? Couldn't voice come from anywhere?

For a bit there is silence at my door. They must be going for help or some kind of … sledgehammer.

I lie down on my bed to rest from the writing. I finger my Swiss Army Knife Elite. I choose one of those littler blades. Without needing to look, I point it straight at my face. With one hand over my Aphonia mouth I carve a tiny smile on my chin. I smile a wide chimp smile. The little carved chin cut stretches and oozes. My soundless mouth above my tiny bleeding mouth. I touch the tiny carved smile with my thumb and smear the warm wet there and put a bloodprint on my wall. I was here. Then I suck my thumb.

I roll over and off of my bed and down to one of the last corners of my wall without my life story on it. I write, "Dear Francis Bacon: the best canvas is the body." I mean, I'm not Francis Bacon. I'm a girl. For sure I can't paint, so I've had to use my body for most everything.

I stare at my girlwalls.

It's taken exactly seventeen purple Sharpies to write my girlstory on these bedroom walls. In the dim light of my orange and purple lava lamp the words make the walls seem to pulse. All those words. I can almost hear them. Nearly no blank wall space left.

I've got until ten p.m. to finish writing and filming this. That's when my ride arrives.

Ass buzz.

I drop to my knees. I smell my Sharpie. I close my eyes. I remember when I was five my mother sat me on her lap while she played franz shoe burt. I know because she said this is franz shoe burt. In my head I repeated the words franz shoe burt. I pictured a guy named burt with beautiful hair and shoes. Long fingers. Even at five I wanted to die sitting in her lap, inside music and the smell of her motherskin and her breasts against my back.

Sitting here huffing my Sharpie on my knees I don't want to open my eyes. Yeah, I know.

It's *Schubert*.

Badaboom. A more potent round of parental authority pounding at the door. Jeez, is that a baseball bat?

Failing.

To.

Penetrate.

I have this weird urge to write Siggy a special note on the wall. Who the hell knows why. It makes my skin itch. Like I owe him a solid one or something. Something like "Don't shit yourself Sig, no way am I giving your wang movie to the slickters." Or "Sig, dude, do not surrender to the Vipermedia Asshats! Resist!" Or maybe what I really want to tell him is "Um, brainbuster? Next time you work with a female? Ask her which city her body is. Or ocean. Give her poetry books written by women. Like Sylvia Plath and Anne Sexton and H.D. and Adrienne Rich and Mary Oliver and Emily Dickinson. Let her draw or paint or sing a self before. You. Say. A. Word.

But I don't write any of those things.

I don't have to. My window is talking. On the other side of my room, tapping on the window that leads to the fire escape, hunched over like a little gargoyle?

Is the Sig.

27.

WITH THE MEMBRANE OF THE WINDOW BETWEEN US, I
put my hand on the glass and look down at him. His breath is
fogging up his side of the window. "Can you hear me?" he
shouts.

I nod.

"I've been trying to reach you!" he yells.

I don't move a muscle. I stare at him.

"Can you please open the window?"

I am a girl statue.

"Ida, for god's sake, can you let me in?" he yells at the glass.

I fog my side of the window with a few big breaths. With
my finger I write backwards: "tell me your dreams."

I watch him read it and then begin to curse. The guy truly
has a case of Tourette's. How does he get on in regular life? Talk
about borderline whack job. I erase my question with my elbow
and refog a space. With my finger I write: "your desire is for
your mother."

He pounds his hand against the glass pretty hard and
hurls some obscenities, but really, he's just an old guy hunched
on a fire escape talking to a minor's window. If a cop drove by?
He'd be so busted. I'm no psychologist, but I know crazy when I
see it. It almost makes me like him.

Behind me there's more commotion. It's possible they will
find a way to break in. I cross my arms over my tits. I take a huge
breath. I let him in.

At first he's all flustered from trying to cram his old-man-balls body in through the fire escape window. But then I get a good look at his face and he looks like utter shit. His eyes are outlined in red and he clearly hasn't slept in a good bit of time. And he's a map of facial tics. He's … well, my diagnosis? He's coked up to the nines.

"Thank god I found you at home," he sputters, all out of breath, his hair even more cuckoo's nest than I'm used to. "I know. I know," he continues, "this is highly unusual, but …"

Um, unusual? Fuck yeah times ten. Once he's in, he shuts the hell up and stares at my walls.

I stare at him staring at my walls. I follow his head as he moves close to one wall, tilts his noggin to the side, stretches out his hand, touches some words. "My god," he whispers.

But then his shoulders jump and he sucks in a wad of old-man air – it's the bedroom door banging again.

"What on earth is that?" he squawks.

My choices for communication at this point are rather endless. I've got enough technology in this room to run a space station. In the end? I decide on the simplest thing of all. "DAD" I write on the palm of my hand, and point it at him. Then I walk over to my desk and grab my laptop. Something tells me this is a sit down. I sit down on my bed. I put the laptop on the bed. I pat the bed on the other side of the laptop and smile.

Sig coughs.

The door pounds.

I open a Word doc. I type, "S'up, doc?"

"Shall I speak?" He asks. His hands are shaking like vibrators.

I shrug. To me, it no longer matters where the voices are coming from. But I do think it's interesting he decides to enter the Word doc.

"Ida," he types.

I immediately snag the laptop back and tap out, "I prefer 'Dora.'"

He stares at it for a second, then types. I can tell he learned to type way back when typewriters existed from how his fingers form into mostly his two forefingers and his hands lift up too high from the keyboard. Almost like a two-fingered pianist. Look at him bang away at those keys. Also he looks a little insane. Why do old dudes always look insane? When he finishes, he hands the laptop to me.

"I lied. About your case study name. The truth is, my sister's nursemaid had to surrender her name when she entered our family. Her name had been 'Rosa.' Rosa was my sister's name. Unless she surrendered her name, she would not have the job. She took the name 'Dora.' When I needed a name for someone who could not keep her real name, 'Dora' is what came to me. My unconscious motivation, I suppose."

I pluck out a few words in response. "You are one fucked-up little dude," I type back and hand to him. I grab the laptop back and type, "So the fuck what?"

Then he types, "You know what I want. I need the video. I'm being hounded like a thief day and night from the media people. If they get their hands on it ... my life is ruined. I must have it."

"Asshats," I type.

"I need that video. Or I need it destroyed. In my presence," he types.

I stare at the Word doc. The cursor blinks its vertical little sly eye.

Then his hands lose motor control and he resorts to speaking. His voice sounds like a skipping record. "I don't ... I have to ... LISTEN ... it's important ..."

I mean wow. He's the epitome of lost-his-marbles old man at this point. He'd be totally right on a dirty street corner down-town asking for change. His pupils look like they are about to dart out of his eyes. Grown-ups really could use some advice on drug use.

Then there's a WHACK at the door that sounds like some-one's skull cracking open. I look at my bedroom door and I'll be

goddamned if whatever they hit it with didn't make – you guessed
it – a VAG crack.

The Sig nearly falls off of the bed, then jumps up and
addresses the door, arms akimbo.

"Now see here," he booms at the door.

"Who the hell is in there?" Pepperoni shrieks back.

"Dr. Freud," Sig answers with authority, suddenly realizing
how weird it is that he's actually in there with me. He shoots me
an uh-oh look. Like I'm supposed to know what to do.

"What are you doing in my daughter's room?" My father
says in a raised-octave voice. It's the voice of a half-father. Weak
and distant and heart attacked. I feel a pang of something
for him inside my ribcage. Once there was Father, wasn't there?

"Now just ease up a minute," Freud stammers. "I can
assure you, I'm here to help. I'm a medical professional."

I look at my Sig reasoning with a door. Arms akimbo.
Really. You crawled through the bedroom of a minor because
you are here to help? Dude. You are so busted! I'm smiling ear to
ear, my freshly cut chin-smile no doubt dribbling blood.

The Sig turns to me and hunches his shoulders and leans
in. "Listen to me," he whisper-spits. "I don't have time for this."
He grabs my arm pretty hard. I look down at my arm where he is
clutching it. "Sorry," he goes. "Just, for the love of christ. Give
me the video, and I'll help you get out of here," he pleads. "What's
wrong with your chin?"

He'll help me? I stare at him inside the womb of my room,
chaos all around us. You know what he looks like? He looks
like what Heidi's grandpa would look like if Heidi's grandpa was
a coked-up loony begging for a fix. I type one last thing on the
laptop and turn it toward him: "Dude. You are a coked-up old
man in the bedroom of a she-minor. Wake up."

All kinds of hell is happening on the other side of my bedroom door. It sounds like the opposite of family. I look at my
half-smashed upside-down digital clock on the floor. It's about
a minute to ten p.m. My ride, I suspect, is here.

Sig's whispering gibberish and chasing me around my room while I pack up. I put my H4n into my Dora purse. Along with my Swiss Army knife. Vicodin. Speedies. Then I walk over to my closet. I rummage around in the shoes I never wear and all the crap that's down there – dirty clothes and dust bunnies and dead batteries and cig butts – in a box in the corner under all that is a trusty tin of lighter fluid and matches. Without even looking at Sig I stand up and point the tin of lighter fluid in his general direction.

"Christ!" he shrieks, and jumps back and away.

I roll my eyes. Holding the tin at hip level I shoot it at my computer. I shoot it all over the floor. I shoot my spray all over the walls, my bed. The smell of camping. Or a family barbecue. My eyes water.

The door is banging and lurching.

Sig is backed against the far wall.

"What in the name of christ are you doing?" he goes.

For a Jew he certainly mouths the word "christ" a lot. What is up with that?

I light a match. I light the matchbook on fire. I throw the flaming matchbook onto my bed.

Instantly there is a bed fireball. Our faces light up and heat. It's really quite stunning, in a pyro, pretty kind of way. The flames make their way out like fingers tracing the lighter-fluid paths I sprayed everywhere.

As the room gets hot as shit I stare at Sig. Right that second? He mirrors me. We have the same look on our faces. The look of "why?" The look you have your whole life, I think. Sometimes words are irrelevant.

But time's shrinking. Things smell like burned apples and synthetic fibers and circuit boards. Sig yells something incomprehensible and drops and rolls. Smoke stings my eyes and skin. My technology begins to crackle and pop. The purple words all over my walls seethe.

For a tiny moment I consider grabbing his arm and pulling

him toward the window ... but you know what? Fuck the Sig. I'm so outta there.

Halfway through the fire escape window, with the Jag, Little Teena, and Ave Maria in sight there on the pavement below me, my bedroom door says one last thing that shocks even me. A booming voice, a voice filled with something from before I was born. It's not my impotent father. It's not Pepperoni. I turn and look back toward the talking door, Sig's deranged little body on the floor behind me just over my shoulder.

"Open the goddamn door you piece-of-shit pervert," the voice booms, "or I'm gonna blow it to smithereens!"

Sig remains grounded on the carpet in a coughing fit.

As I clamber down the fire escape toward freedom I realize whose voice was at the door. Late, but not never.

My mother's.

28.

WHEN SHE OPENS HER APARTMENT DOOR, MARLENE
wears a black Nike warm-up suit and bright purple Nikes. Bright
purple nails. Bright purple eye shadow. She brings a big black
Nike sports bag with everything else we need into the kitchen.

First things first: the wigs. For Little Teena, AKA "the
caseworker," a man's curly number with mutton chops. And a
furry black mustache. For Ave Maria, AKA "the distraught
sister," an Alice in Wonderland complete with baby blue head-
band. Eerily wholesome. And for me, AKA "teen gone wrong,"
no wig. My hair has hit the length of girls who cut their own
hair short in little self-destructive hacking motions. I look exactly
like a girl who fucked up her own head and life. I don't need a
wig. I'm perfect for me.

We could SO be on an episode of *The First 48*.

Ave Maria rummages around in the Nike sports bag
looking for extra "disguise" crap. She pulls out an eyepatch.
"Can I wear an eyepatch too?" She straps it on. Now she looks
like a pirate Alice in Wonderland.

"Why not," Little Teena goes. "We can pretend Dora lost it
and stabbed you in the eye." He begins to glue down his mutton
chops.

I rub my mangy head. I could probably pass for a guy. But
I don't want to be a guy.

The Farrah wig from before is at the ready. For later. After we retrieve Obsidian from the godforsaken teen halfway house hell. For the airport. I carefully fold it and stow it in my backpack.

Marlene leaves the kitchen for a moment and returns with a soft pelt in her arms. "This," she says very solemnly, "is for your Obsidian." A hush falls over us all. We stare at the monumental beauty of it. A Wonder Woman wig. Big huge piles of dark chocolate locks. Then Marlene carefully explains the postescape drama to me.

By the time we get to Sea-Tac Airport – assuming we get that far – Obsidian and I will have become two young hair show models on their way to Paris for one of the most important hairdressing industry conferences around. For those who are in search of excellence, who are always looking ahead for ways to innovate in the growing industry of hair design, this conference is a cross between the best in artistry and the best in business, featuring the top names in hair, creators who believe in a new you for every age. Marlene hands me several brochures.

False IDs, false paperwork, false hair.

Courtesy of Hakizamana Ojo.

It doesn't matter who you really are in the world any longer. It only matters what it says on your documents and what the rules of surveillance are on your chosen path. Houston means take off any twat or tit jewelry or you'll be strip-searched. O'Hare means add three hours to your wait-in-line time and don't even think about trying to act "down" by saying "da bomb" or anything. If you have the right documentation for the particular geographic area, the right magical stamps and data and weird little tilt and glow hieroglyphics on your paperwork and identification, you can be anyone. I know the current shtick is that HOMELAND SECURITY is all over your ass, but you know what the truth is? The folks manning the security at airports are all a bunch of overworked underpaid people who just need paychecks and jobs so they don't get deported or arrested or thrown out of their homes.

Ironic, isn't it?

The paperwork is neatly displayed before us on Marlene's

kitchen table. It really is something. Artful even. I take out my purple Sharpie. I write "BEAUTIFUL" on the surface of Marlene's kitchen table. She smiles.

"Now I have something to remember you by," she says.

My chest implodes.

It's time to go. My arms go numb. My mouth opens. I drop my head down and look at the linoleum floor. So I don't have to think about not seeing Marlene for god knows how long I study the floor. When I look back up, Marlene is all business.

"I will meet you at my north terminal surveillance hut," Marlene says, winking, and hands me two plane tickets. She sizes me and my little sadness up. "Liebchen!" she says. "This is not the last time you will see me. Of that I am certain. This is simply the last time we will see each other as the people we are in this kitchen this moment."

She laughs. You know which laugh. The one from her belly. The one with all of history in it.

"Think who you will be the next time! We will drink to it!" she exclaims.

"Yay!" Ave Maria pipes, spinning around in a circle, her real hair shooting out like spaghetti.

I want Marlene's laugh to hold us like that all night – in her kitchen – wigs all over the place – the word "BEAUTIFUL" drawn in purple Sharpie on her kitchen table. I walk over to her and hug her and bury my face in her tits, wondering even inside my ripped-up heart what her tits are made of. Socks? Silicone? They feel like perfect warm water balloons against my face.

When we leave the back of my head itches. I'm afraid to turn back around and look or I'll bawl like a pussy.

But Marlene calls out in a booming manwoman voice, "Lamskotelet!" So I gotta turn around one last time.

In Marlene's hand is a giant plastic bag filled with bacon. "For the journey!" And laughing and laughing.

29.

IN THE JAG ON THE WAY TO THE TEEN HALFWAY HOUSE
I stare at my thighs. Then I stare out the car window. Shadows
of shit pass by. It's late. Maybe midnight. We want to control the
scene at the halfway house. We're hoping for a small staff of
exhausted underpaid workers. I'm riding shotgun.

Little Teena, AKA "the caseworker," drives. His face is
partially lit up by the green and orange console lights. Ave Maria,
AKA "the distraught sister," is in the back seat. I can see her head
bopping up and down in the rear view mirror. Her earbuds
jammed in her ears. Her Alice in Wonderland hair cascading over
her shoulder. Her absurd eyepatch momentarily flipped up.

I think into the night. I search the sky. I used to be able to
find the Dippers easily. Now I don't know what direction to look.

No one says anything, especially me.

It hurts. The silence.

We drive.

I think I see some cows pass by on the side of the road but
they might just be those eye blotches you get when you are trying
not to cry.

Mercifully, Little Teena saves me from my own pathos.

"All right. What's our motivation?" he shouts out.

Ave Maria pulls out her earbuds. "What?" she says.

"Our motivations. We need to know how to act," he repeats.

"Oh. Did we eat all the bacon?" Ave Maria says, hooking her
arms over the seat so her face is up by us in the front.

I hand her what's left of the bacon. The whole car pretty much smells like pig oil.

Between swine chews Ave Maria says, "Well, I'm beside myself because my sister tried to gouge my eye out with a … with a …" she looks up at the felted car ceiling, "with a spoon!" she says.

I have to admit, I like it. That girl has hidden talents. God knows I've always got a spoon with me. My mother's.

"But you love your sister too, isn't that right, distraught sister? You can't bear for anything too terrible to happen to her?" Little Teena coaches.

"Uh huh!" Ave Maria agrees, chewing seriously.

"I'm the sole legal guardian, is what the paperwork says," Ave Maria goes.

I smile. I am never going to meet anyone like her in my life again. I know it.

"I'm wanting outta this chickenshit assignment – bucking for a reassignment – homicide. I'm looking to make detective." He fingers a mutton chop. He waves his finger at us collectively and says, "You two are an embarrassment to me. Beneath me. I'm just looking to unload you," he points to me, "and bone you," he points to Ave Maria, "before it's all over."

Ave Maria cracks up. I do too. The image of Little Teena AKA the mutton-chopped caseworker boning little miss eyepatch while the scary bald teen tries to gouge everyone's eyes out with a spoon is worthy of an LSD dose.

"So then let's go over the script again," Little Teena prods.

"I know what to say," Ave Maria bleats, nearly hitting her head on the car ceiling. "I'm supposed to make a big deal all distraught-y if we need a … what do you call it?"

"Diversion." Little Teena shakes his head up and down.

"You say all the cop-ly stuff and give whoever is at the intake desk that whole cool pile of paperwork. Do you wanna practise your cop-y authority voice on us?" Ave Maria's quite nearly in the front seat with us, her skinny arms and elbows poking everywhere.

Little Teena clears his throat. "We've got a live one here, I'm afraid, emergency intake. They can't take her up at Chelan so we had to come here. Full up at Chelan. Christ. Kids these days, huh?"

"Fuck, that's hot!" Ave Maria shouts. "Say it again!"

Little Teena complies. Then they go back and forth for a bit in mock bad cop television show lingo. It's weirdly relaxing.

I look out of the car window again. I push the button and my window goes down. The night air hits my face. I close my eyes. So much like a dream, things are sometimes. Or a movie. If I was filming us driving I'd put a Nick Cave song in. I'd zoom in on ordinary objects in the car – Little Teena's thick fingers on the steering wheel, the green glow of the speedometer and digital clock. Ave Maria's Hot Tamales sticking out of the pocket of her jean jacket. And the pink plastic of my Dora purse – the safety pins for eyes – my black skinny jeans knees. It's a claustrophobic little world the objects we own make for us.

But then I'd pan out to the view beyond the inside of the car, because you can do that with film – you can expand or contract space – you can trick time by going slow motion so that a few seconds of silence riding in a car lasts thirty minutes. You can speed up an entire day and night so it looks like a series of retinal flashes.

If I was filming this scene I'd go from the vastness of a night sky back to each of our faces there in the car – the way faces close up can look like their own universes. Ave Maria's eyes are blue-green. Like the ocean. Little Teena has a cool little comma scar just under his right eye. It makes him look perpetually shy just under his badassery. My face is like a blank screen to me. I don't know what there is about my face. Sometimes I'm scared it's nothing.

My ass buzzes. I pull it out. It's a text. *Ida, please call me*. Mother.

"Let's just go over the steps again," Little Teena says.

"Yay!" Ave Maria goes.

I laugh but nothing sounds.

"Step one. Enter and distract intake person. Me at desk, Ave Maria hanging back with spooky sister."

"Check!" Ave Maria sings.

"Step two. Engage script and hand over paperwork to move toward entrance."

"Check!" An octave higher.

"Step three. Gain entrance, knock the intaker in the head from behind, get Obsidian."

"Double check!" Ave Maria operatically sings, then says, "Can I hit the whoever it is with a Coke bottle? There's an old-school Coke bottle back here – my mom loves this little Mexican market where they sell the old-school Coke bottles." She holds it up. "Aren't they cute? They're little!"

I look over at Little Teena. Then back at Ave Maria. They continue their fake dialogue and their step rehearsals in their fake hair in Ave Maria's mom's Jag. Love isn't what you were ever expecting. I open my mouth. Nothing comes out. No voice, I mean. I smile. Little Teena interprets the silence correctly. Ave Maria pets my sketchy hair. I shove the last of the bacon in my mouth. It's salty and rubbery yet crisp. What is bacon but fat and gristle and thin strips of ass meat?

Tastes like … family.

30.

THE HALFWAY HOUSE LOOKS LIKE ONE OF THOSE GROUP
homes for the non-neurotypical. You've seen them, usually a
two-story dingy dark gray number with security bars on the
windows and doors and dead grass for a yard contained by a
crappy-ass chainlink fence.

This one has what looks like a tall surveillance mechanism
posted sentry-like near the entrance, but on closer inspection?
It's just a goddamn bug zapper.

"Google Earth it," Ave Maria says from the back seat of the
Jag.

Little Teena does. We're parked about two blocks away.
We put our three heads together in the back of the Jag and study
the halfway house on the laptop. Pretty much one way in and
out. Through the front. Though fire code probably means there's
a back door. It's the law. It's bad to let teens burn up. Hard to
get social services funding if you, you know, barbecue them. So
there must be a back exit.

I delete my mother and text on my cell to Little Teena: *Can
you hack in? Surveillance?*

Christ. It looks like somebody's big huge crackhouse.

Little Teena taps away at the laptop keyboard. Bless the
fingers of Little Teena. He chuckles. "All they've got going on is
like a series of nanny cams. And electronic locks that are ...
lemme see ... ha. Morons. The electronic locks are all controlled

at the front desk. They've got a password tumbler from like the *Starsky and Hutch* years." He continues typing code.

"Why, it's just a dumbass little meanness hotel!" Ave Maria pipes.

"Oh my fucking god," Little Teena says. "Their password? Get this. Their password is … PASSWORD. I can unlock everything from here and disable their idiotic 'safety system' without them even knowing it. Fucking figures. Department of Juvenile Justice? I salute you!" Little Teena salutes the air. "Dumb douches."

Before we leave the car, I text them both: *Hatha breathing*. They know because I taught them. We all close our eyes and hold hands. We breathe in for seven seconds. We hold it for seven seconds. We breathe out for seven seconds. We picture the ocean. We do it seven times. When we open our eyes, we are our characters.

As we walk toward the entrance I can hear bugs die zap deaths in the bug zapper. My role is of course to look troubled, dejected, like I might lash out.

Tough gig, huh.

Little Teena carries his air of authority, his clipboard, his fake wad of papers.

Ave Maria fiddles with her eyepatch. I slap her hand away from her face. "Sorry," she goes, and then sports a distraught sister face so fast it takes my breath away. Right before we get to the entrance, Ave Maria grabs both of our arms and whisper-sings, "You guys? You guys rock!" Then she kisses each of our hands and immediately returns to her role. She's gonna make an awesome mom some day.

Upon entering it's clear that "intake" is bogus. Some fat-ass guy in a white man jumpsuit with – I shit you not – a box of half-eaten powdered donuts is at the front desk. The computer system? Dell. You heard me. What kind of a monkeyfuck operation is this? Dell computers? This is going to be like taking candy from geriatrics.

Little Teena assesses the situation about as quickly as I do, and launches smoothly into his spiel. "Got an emergency intake on a transport from Bellevue. They can't take her up at Chelan so we had to come here. Full up at Chelan. Christ. Kids these days, huh?" Little Teena jabs the exquisite pile of false paperwork and the clipboard at the fat-ass.

So far everything is proceeding according to the steps.

"I didn't get any call about an intake tonight. You just hold on here," fatty blabs. He's got powdered sugar on his upper lip. Man, you can't make this shit up.

"Who's this?" Blubbo says, pointing at Ave Maria.

Little Teena leans over the counter and points to the data on the fake forms that identifies Ave Maria as "next of kin" and "sister" and "legal guardian." "Parents are dead," Little Teena explains. "How these two managed to keep out of child custody services all these years is beyond me. But that one?" Little Teena points at Ave Maria. He leans over the desk and whispers to whale boy. "She's a nurse. Candy-striper." And then he winks at intake balloon.

I stand there trying to look as silently dangerous as possible. I shoot for a kind of Bob De Niro in *Taxi Driver* look. I smile, then go cold-faced, then smile again. I spit on the floor and then for no reason I whistle "When You Wish Upon a Star".

Everyone turns and stares at me for a minute.

"See what I mean?" Little Teena says. "We've got a live one. Do me a favor and take this little teen monster girl off my hands, will ya? Mind?" he says, moving in to snag a donut.

"I don't know, I just don't know ... this is highly irregular," puffy says, shuffling through the paperwork, but the paperwork is jake. Marlene is a pro. Nothing is missing. Everything has the proper signature or seal or whacked-out institutional code lingo all over it. I shoot a glance up at a surveillance camera in the back corner behind the human blimp. I smile and pick my nose. I nonchalantly flip on my Zoom H4n.

"It's just highly irregular," he says again. He picks up the phone. "I'm gonna have to call it in downtown."

You know that sound in the movie soundtrack where the record needle skips and drives a wedge through the album? It's the oh fuck soundscape.

Ave Maria, no doubt improvising, begins to cry. It's a unique weeping, of course. Little hiccup-sounding whimper lurches. He stares at her, phone in the air between his gut and his ear. Then she amps up the crying and starts this rather impressive erratic breathing thing. Her face gets blotchy. She scratches at the sides of her own arms. I swear she could do performance art.

"Oh shit," Little Teena says, "you don't wanna upset this one," he says, following her lead, stroking one of his lamb chops.

I grit my teeth menacingly.

"Wait a minute here, wait a minute," the gut says, standing up, one hand on his ... what the fuck is that? Yeah. Should have guessed. Taser.

I spit.

Little Teena starts to walk around the intake desk where blubberino is. "You better listen to me or we're gonna have a situation here," Little Teena says. He moves behind the desk.

"Hey!" White Fat Albert exclaims, "You can't come back here!"

Ave Maria shoots for a major distraction and turns the volume up to full wail. "If there's no room here, what are you going to do to my siiiiiiiiiiissssssssssssster? You can't put her in jail! Please don't put her in jail! She can't go to JJJJJJJJJAAAAAAAA-IIIIIILLLLLLLLL," wailing and bawling full force – until she's pretty much textbook ... what's the word I'm searching for? Oh yeah. Hysterical.

"What the ..." chub says, "hey, can you get her to quiet down? We've got a houseful of sensitives here – hey! Can you get her to stop that?"

Ave Maria is rocking and crying and pulling her Alice hair, making a total scene.

Little Teena's nearly next to lard-ass behind the intake desk. I start jumping up and down like a bunny.

"Which one of 'em did you say was the live one?" fatty goes, his eyes big blue buttons.

"The head case," Little Teena says, pointing at me. I bite my lip until it bleeds and smile.

"That other's her sister," Little Teena yells above the ruckus Ave Maria is making, "like I said. Legal guardian, if you can believe it. Sister nearly got her eye put out – but still wouldn't let us take her without coming along. Families, huh? Buncha crackpots if you ask me."

"Well, all right, all right," donut face says, and punches some-thing into his Dell. Then he gets on some kind of walkie talkie device. Like a Toys 'R' Us-looking walkie talkie. Budget cuts? Christ this place has the technology of *Sesame Street*.

Pudgeball speaks some mysterious lingo into his Toys 'R' Us walkie talkie. Something equally incomprehensible comes back out at him. "I know what time it is. We got an emergency kinda thing down here. We got an immediate intake. We can sort it out in the morning. Get your ass out of bed." Gibberish white noise comes back.

It begins to look like things are back on track.

"All righty then we're gonna set her up temporarily in a room here," pudding says, licking his fingers, "but we'll need a transfer in the morning. This is a one-night deal. I don't care who signed your paperwork, we're full up. Got a wetback last night that tried to bite me. Man, they just don't pay me enough for this shit."

My.

Breathing.

Jackknifes.

Wetback. This dumb racist motherfucker thinks Obsidian is Mexican. My heart fists my chest. I clench my hands into little bomblets. Little Teena feels me ramping up and shoots me an easy-now look. "Yeah, well I'm sure you get all kinds," Little Teena says. "Say, did you intake that barefoot bandit dude? I heard he ended up in these parts?"

"Naw, we ain't that lucky. We just get the real rejects. Had to restrain that wetback. Tight. She's a looker though," he says, rubbing his third chin and laughing, "wouldn't mind a tap or two, if you know what I mean … but hell. I need this job."

There is a bomb in my skull. An IED. This guy? This guy has got to go.

Little Teena is shooting me just-calm-down looks.

You know how sometimes your actual brain gets taken over by your … id? Pretty sure that's the correct terminology. The image of this fat-ass fuck restraining Obsidian and leaning over her with his three chins and chub sweat and donut drool snaps my brain into little black shards of id. And you know what they say about the id. It's a cauldron of seething excitations striving solely to bring about the satisfaction of instinctual needs.

Guess who I learned that from?

So when fat boy turns to me and says, "You got a name, ugly?"

Fuck the plan.

I step up to his intake desk. Particle board painted white. I'll tell you who I am, I say in my head. I'm an id-ridden ball of chaos, motherfucker. I'm your worst nightmare. My eyes feel a little like they are going to shoot out of my head and shatter his face into a zillion pieces. I open my mouth. And then

My.

Throat.

Flaps.

BANG.

Voice.

"YEAH," I go, much to the surprise of Little Teena and Ave Maria, and maybe even me. "I have a name, assfuck. My name is Dora," I say, and then I lurch across his pathetic little desk and bite his cheek exactly like a chimp mauling its so-called human parent would.

31.

"GET HER OFF ME GET HER OFF!" THE HUMAN PUFFER-fish screams.

I taste metal. Chub's blood.

Then I see rainbow lightning? No, it's Crazy String–you know, that kid crap you shoot out of a can–being shot all over the place, no doubt by a one-eyed blond girl who is piping high notes all over the room. Before I can say, "Where the fuck did you get Crazy String?" Ave Maria gets hold of a hand-held bullhorn from tubby the tubs' desk–you know, the kind that make the ear-piercing BLAP noise.

BLAP!

And

BLAP!

I swear those things could give you a heart attack.

Lardo struggles away from my monkey attack. I froth and growl.

"Just what the fuck is going on here?" he screams, cupping his newly gnawed-on cheek, striking a defensive fat-boy pose.

Little Teena deftly dips in and snags the Taser right off of chub butt's hip holster. Momentarily deafened from the BLAP, also bleeding from the meat of his cheek, also blinded by Crazy String wrapped all over his face and head, intake guy gets three Taser shots from Little Teena straight to the gut. Fatty slaps at the air and then falls out of his chair onto the floor, making a little "maaaaaawwwwrrrrllll" sound.

"He's Tased, bro!" Ave Maria pipes, jumping up and down.

Undeterred and seemingly in control, Little Teena rummages around in the desk drawers. Duct tape is in there like it was waiting for us. He chucks it at me. "Mouth, wrists, ankles," he shouts, wielding the Taser like a Glock. Man, mutton chops just look right on him. It's a little disturbing.

I'm pretty much deaf from the BLAP horn too, but I know what to do. Mouth, wrists, ankles. Oh jeez. Blubbo has cankles. While I'm taping Godzilla up, Little Teena climbs a chair and fiddles with the security camera.

"What are you doing?" I go. But then I get it. Duh. He's taking out the SD card. Now we'll have a film of ourselves. Brilliant.

But this whole scene has ramped up from zero to sixty pretty fucking fast. I am sweating under my tits and on my upper lip. Fuck. Think straight. Then someone's tugging on my arm from below. Ave Maria? Little Teena? Security?

I turn. I look down amidst the chaos. But who is there just isn't possible. Unless you think about all the ways in which we ditch people we don't want to deal with. I'll be goddamned. I mean I'll be double, triple goddamned.

It's Smiley from the hospital! Smiling the too-smiley from ear to ear, tugging on my sleeve.

"Smiley?" I go. "What the fuck are you doing here?"

"GULL!" Smiley responds, and claps, and points to the door between us and the incarcerated juvies. Little Teena blows the tip of the Taser like it's smoking, spins it in his hand, then drops it to the floor.

"Um, any chance you can open that?" I ask Smiley, pointing to the door leading to the rest of the house.

"Don't," Ave Maria coos, "he's just—"

Smiley coughs. "Why, I certainly can," he says, as plain as day.

I stare at him for a long few seconds. Ave Maria stares at him. Little Teena smiles. The only thing that makes Smiley sound different from you or me? A slightly thickened tongue.

"You sly motherfucker," I gush. "What's your name?" I ask.

"Oedipus," he goes, complete with a hand flourish and head bow.

"No fucking shit?" I go.

He stares at me like I'm an idiot. "My name is Ted." And then he smiles the smile of a comrade in arms. He spins and wheels over to the safety door.

"It's real good to meet you, Ted," I say, and put my hand on his shoulder. "Do you mind if I ask, do you work here, or are you ..."

"An inmate?" he goes over his shoulder. He nods his head up and down, then says, "And we've met before. At the hospital?"

"Yeah, I know," I go, looking at the top of his head, "it's just that the last time I saw you, you were kinda being chased like you'd escaped some kind of ..."

"Nut house?"

I stand in silence as Ave Maria and Little Teena move up behind us.

"I guess you could call me an escape artist," Smiley says, "particularly when I'm off my meds. That day in the hospital? Off my meds. The rest of the time they keep me pretty much anesthetized."

"Whud ju do?" Ave Maria asks.

"Set fire to my foster parents' house," he says.

I'm not sure but I think we are looking at him like we pity him.

"Were they creeps?" Little Teena ventures.

"You could say that," Smiley says without looking at us.

As Smiley locates the right key on a gigantic metal key chain he's got stashed to the side of his wheel, he says, "Only one thing pisses me off though." He punches the key into the lock.

"What's that?" Little Teena goes.

"That barefoot bandit fucker? The one that broke out of all the juvie homes and stole boats and planes and shit? That little brat got all the coverage. Good-looking son of a bitch too.

Nobody gives a shit about us differently abled anymore. They don't even cover Special Olympics hardly. And that wheelchair hundred-yard dash? That fucker was so mine. We're old news."

"Sucks," Ave Maria sings.

"Yeah," he says, crouching over the door knob from his wheelchair and opening the door between us and Obsidian. "Man, you'd be amazed how much bawling and blubbering it takes to convince people you are witless." He shoots a look over at our duct-taped Moby Dick over on the floor where we left him. "We better hurry. I've been Tased before and he's gonna come out of that in about two minutes."

"Jesus," I say, looking at Ted. I clutch my throat. My throat that recently banged out a voice. I feel a kind red itch between us. That smile. The wailing GULL sounds. A kid whose parents let him down. He's the perfect con man for our times.

Or just my teen id hero.

"C'mon," Smiley says, holding the door open by jamming his wheelchair against it, "your friend's through here."

32.

I HURL AND HURL. I'M A BARFING HEAD OUT OF THE window of a speeding Jag. What the fuck just happened?

I blow pumpkin-color monkey chunks all over the side of the car. Sorry Ave Maria's mom. Everything smells like bile and spit and girl puke. My head feels like a hard metal pinball has gotten loose. THINK. PLAYBACK.

The movie in my head starts with us going to Obsidian's room to spring her. Obsidianobsidianobsidian. Black shard of glass. Biceped beauty. My ears hot. Dizzy. Smiley opening the door. When we embrace, everything I've ever known supernovas. Just our mouths and heads and bodies. Just heat and her black hair and her skin smelling like rain. Just my ribs spreading like wings.

I wipe my mouth. Cold night air beats my head up outside the window of the Jag. Ave Maria is petting my neck. Obsidian has her leg crossed over mine. Like she's trying to keep me from blowing a hole through the top of the car.

Marlene.

My head movie returns. We were making our exit. Smiley popping wheelies down the long hall toward the back of the building. Through some kitchen that smelled like SpaghettiOs. Then a booming authority voice behind us at the other end of the hall. The voice of all parents or cops or lawyers or gym teachers.

"IDA," it shouts. "STOP," it shouts. "We have something of yours."

I turn around. Not cops.

Even undercover cops don't have suits with thread count that high.

It's silverslick the agent and two goons – but that's not all. It's Marlene with a Taser jammed up against her neck. Her wrists and mouth duct-taped. Marlene in a vintage 50s hoop skirt and the hair of Zsa Zsa Gabor.

I lean further out of the window and watch the knotty pavement zip by beneath us. I don't even know where the fuck we are. Bum-fuck Washington. My throat ouches and my head pounds. I consider jumping out of the window of a moving Jag.

Marlene.

Did I leave her there?

Is this coming of age?

The authority voice going, "Give us the video and we'll let this faggot go."

In my gut, fire. Napalm.

Marlene's eyes going run. Marlene's eyes going get the hell out of here. Marlene in my head as a young boy running, running all the way to America.

The authority voice going, "Give us your media."

Me and the posse up against the silverfucks. I turn to Obsidian Ave Maria Little Teena Smiley I go, "run." They don't move. I yell, "FUCKING RUN." They do. Out of the building.

In the Jag Ava Maria says to me quietly, "Sugar, um, your butt is buzzing."

I don't move. Snot runs down my lips. My eyes puff up. "I know. It's my fucking mother," I croak.

"Oh," Ave Maria says, "then want me to chuck it out the window?" She's still got her goddamn eyepatch on.

"Let's everyone just calm the fuck down," Little Teena says from the driver's seat. His wig has shot off his skull but is held to his face by the glued-on mutton chops. Surreal.

Marlene. My head movie plays it over and over. Marlene with Tasers jammed up against her throat and ribs and gut.

The authority voice yelling, "Give us the media or this perv gets a high voltage shave." Then he rips off the duct tape. That awful scraped-off skin sound.

Oh fuck. Fuck. My head movie is some god-awful B-movie thriller. I slide my Dora purse off my shoulder and put it on the floor between me and them. I make like I'm gonna kick it down the hall to them. You could say everything I am is in that little pink vag bag.

The name "Taser?" It's an acronym for Thomas A. Swift's Electric Rifle. A young adult novel written by Victor Appleton. Marlene told me that.

In my head movie next Marlene's voiceover takes over. Not talking. Laughing. Deep and rumbly it starts off, confusing the goons. Then she brings the laugh to a hearty howl, then a roar, then a thunder, her mouth so wide open she could swallow a head. Her laugh vibrates the walls and floors. The goons punch her torso. Her breasts go ajar. Her laugh shakes the ceiling the linoleum floor the faces of the goons. She laughs Rwanda.

Of course I want her to shut the fuck up and save herself but I also want her laugh to blow up the building.

I close my eyes and bawl like a girl. Obsidian is trying to pull my head back into the Jag. My butt is buzzing and buzzing. Little Teena turns the radio on. Even at two a.m. they do the news on NPR.

"Oh jeez," Ave Maria says.

I pull my head back in.

On the radio – it's Michele Norris. They've got the Sig. A prominent Seattle psychiatrist arrested at a possible arson scene. A teen is missing from the residence.

Could this night get anymore fucking fucked? My ass again.

Obsidian digs the buzzing iPhone out from my back pocket.

"You're right. It's your mom. She wants to talk to you. Bad," she says.

"No shit," I go. "Well, I'm not calling her." I blow my nose in the sleeve of my hoodie, then roll the sleeve up over the slime.

My voice quivers like a pussy's. "I'm not calling my goddamn mother."

"Maybe she knows whether or not we're an all points bulletin," Little Teena says.

"Cool!" Ave Maria sings before she can stop herself.

"It's not funny," Little Teena says, shooting a goddamn-it look at Ave Maria. Then he says, "Are those fuckers tailing us? Who were they?"

Ave Maria climbs from the front seat to the back and then nearly into the space between the back window and the seat – where dogs go. "I don't see anyone," she says.

"I stabbed all their tires when we ran out," Obsidian mumbles.

No one says anything but we are glad. I stare at the shard of obsidian hanging from her neck.

Ave Maria climbs back over to the front seat, then turns around and hooks her elbows over the seat, looking back at me and Obsidian. "Do you think Marlene is ... like, all burned or something?" Her voice is whispery and grave. Little Teena coughs. I stare at Ave Maria hard enough to take her head off. She wilts. "I just meant ..."

"Just shut it," Little Teena growls at her.

I don't mean to, but I grab Ave Maria's pencil-thin wrists. Then I squeeze. I squeeze harder. Her eyes widen but she doesn't make a sound. Harder. She grits her teeth. I squeeze so hard I'm pretty sure I could snap her hands off of her arms. Still she makes no sound. She just locks eyes with me. Finally Obsidian says, "Enough," quietly against my neck. She puts her hands on my hands. I let go.

Ave Maria turns around in the passenger seat and drops her head.

When they jam Thomas Swift's Electric Rifle into Marlene's throat and ribs and gut the megawatt electricity shoots her head up and back and her arms fly out to her sides ripping the duct tape and her torso stiffens and arches with voltage. But she's still laughing. Her chest heaves and her laugh becomes monstrous and I think I see electricity shooting from her hair, her eyes, her ajar tits, her mouth, her nostrils, her fingers, electricity shooting out in a radius around her, the laughing ringing my bones and heart but then from behind me I hear "GULLLL!!!" and it's Smiley shooting past me and grabbing my Dora bag off the floor and pitching it to me as he wheels by and picks up speed heading straight for them until he crashes into the horrible electric trinity that is Marlene and the silverfucks and the snap and smell of current shakes my skin and Little Teena is pulling me into a dead run. That's the last image. That's the end of the film in my head.

Marlene.

Lit up.

In the Jag I stare at the back of Little Teena's head. Obsidian takes her shirt off and wipes my face. Then sits there shirtless like it's normal. No one says anything. I feel like a human three-day-old shitty tampon of a person. We need somewhere to go. I close my eyes.

"OK," I go. "I'll call my mom."

33.

ON THE OTHER END OF MY IPHONE MY MOM SOUNDS like a tin mother.

I know things about technology. Like a cellphone is an electronic device used for full duplex two-way radio telecommunications over a cellular network of base stations known as base sites. In addition to being a telephone, modern mobile cells also support text messages, email, Internet access, gaming, Bluetooth, infrared, camera, MMS, MP3 player, radio, and GPS.

Parents don't know shit about cellphones.

"We need somewhere to go," I say quietly to the tin mother.

"Ida," she says.

I hold the iPhone out the car window and let the rushing cold air nearly take it from my palm. I close my eyes. Briefly I want to open the car door and jump out. The end.

I don't know how to talk to this person. I rack my brain for something to say that doesn't feel like a chunka puke. When I return the iPhone to my ear I say, "Do you remember the first time you played me franz shoe burt?"

After a long silence she says, "Yes, Ida. You were five, I think. You sat on my lap."

Right answer. Does that mean something? Anything? Are you my mother?

"Where are you?" I ask.

On her end I hear classical music. I hear a mother humming to her child. I hear a child laughing. No.

It's just a television.

"I'm at a Holiday Inn just outside of Kelso."

"Oh," I go.

Then it's just us sucking in and blowing out air into our cellphones. I can hear her breathing. She can hear mine. We don't breathe alike, as near as I can tell. I try to match hers. A kid thing.

"Why Holiday Inn?" I go.

"Are you all right?" she asks.

"How was Vienna?" I say.

Dead air. Television backdrop.

"I have something for you," she says.

My voice comes out all in a rush. "For the longest time I thought it was the word 'shoe,' and the word 'burt.' Isn't that dumb? I used to imagine a guy with great footwear and beautiful hands … Isn't that the stupidest fucking thing you've ever heard?" I say into my iPhone. I look at Obsidian. In her eyes there is something like a mirror. I see a girl leaving my own face, and someone I've never known replacing her.

"Room 324," the tin mother goes.

"Tomorrow is my birthday," I say, but my voice is unrecognizable to me.

"I know, Ida," she whispers, signaling through the flames.

34.

THEY DON'T TELL YOU LOVE CAN SNEAK UP ON YOUR ASS
and sucker-punch you.

When my mother opens the door of Room 324 of the Holiday
Inn she looks like what Catherine Deneuve would look like if
Catherine Deneuve loved you unconditionally. And if Catherine
Deneuve loved you unconditionally? Trust me, you'd swoon.

Catherine Deneuve's real name was Catherine Fabienne
Dorléac.

I fight the swoon with all my might. I grab Obsidian's hand
so we're two-fisted. My mother stares at our hands and takes
it in. She looks up and collects Ave Maria and Little Teena in her
gaze, too. She stands aside and lets us all in to the hotel room
like it's in her nature. The room smells like a mother's perfume,
a little like vodka, a little like bath salts. Clothes sit neatly folded
in a black suitcase, the lid open. Toiletries stand guard over
by the sink, neatly. The carpet is the color of dirt. The bedspread
and drapes' pattern a combination of dirt and ochre colors.
There is a painting of horses on the wall. A crappy painting. The
television bubbles. News. When I look at the bed I see a slightly
rumpled hollow where a single woman has been there watching
TV and drinking alone. I don't see any pill bottles but they must
be here somewhere.

"Oh GAWD this room is so dreamy!" Ave Maria chirps,
throwing herself onto the mother bed, caving in instantaneously.
Typical.

My mother mans the remote control and points our attention in the direction of the nightly news. It's us. The nightly news is us. Sort of. There's been an arrest of a well-known psycho-analyst. A missing girl. A fire in a Seattle condo. An incident at a juvenile halfway house up north. The news reporter on scene at the halfway house is interviewing an eye-witness. There is a short clip of Ted. "MAWR," he bellows, and sucks his hand. Local authorities are investigating.

Gee, other than that, we're free and clear.

"Christ," Little Teena says.

"There's no mention of Marlene," I say to Little Teena. "Or the showbiz goons."

"I noticed," he goes.

Obsidian comes up behind me and spoons me and says, "She got away, I'm sure of it."

My stomach feels pretty much like I swallowed cement and my bunghole is forever encased in stone. I feel dizzy. I sit on the edge of the dirt-brown and ochre bed and put my head between my legs. What are they going to do to Ted? Is Sig in jail? And where in the hell is Marlene? Alive? Dead? All because of me? "Fucking fuck …" I exhale.

A hand rests on my shoulder. I clamp on it – thinking it's Obsidian – but right away I feel the wedding ring and elastic skin so soft skin and realize it's her. My mother.

"Ida," she says.

I look up and straighten up and shoot a defiant look upwards. "My name is Dora now," I say.

"I see," she says. Not even fazed. "Dora, then."

I stand up and pace the room. I don't look at her. I try not to smell her skin lotion or bath salts or vodka breath, all of which feel familiar as a teddy bear to me. I try not to want to touch her waves of hair. I try not to remember sitting in her lap and wanting to die there. "I have a plan," I stammer. "Obsidian and I just need to get to the airport is all. We have … wigs."

"Wigs?" My mother crosses her arms over her chest. She

is wearing a black cotton turtle neck and black straight-leg jeans. She looks like a pretty middle-aged Catherine Deneuve spymom. "Dora," she says, clearing her throat, "may I speak to you alone? In the bathroom?"

Ave Maria grabs a hotel pillow and covers her head and ears with it. Little Teena proceeds to fix himself a drink. Obsidian looks at me with "if you want we can run" in her eyes.

Every part of me doesn't want to speak alone in the bathroom. Except for of course my entire self, who just once wants more than oxygen to get to be alone with this beautiful spymom. To bury my face in her chest. To have her hold me and rock me like a tiny fucking baby and sing to me and FUCK. GODDAMN IT. GET A GRIP, PUSSY.

"Fine. Whatever." I stomp into the bathroom.

Once we're in there, my mother unbuttons her pants and pulls her pants and underwear down and pees. A great waterfall of gushing piss. I mean my mom's vag is in full view. I stare at the sink.

"Oh gaaaaawwwwwwwd," she moans. "I held that too long."

I bite the inside of my cheek so I don't say what I'm thinking, which is doesn't that feel kind of orgasmically good?

My mother finishes peeing and stands up. The room smells briefly like very pretty bums. Then she flushes and sits on the edge of the bathtub. I lean against the closed bathroom door with my arms crossed over my chest. I stare at the shower head.

"Ida – I mean, Dora," she goes, "this is a little awkward."

No shit.

I sneak a peek at her face briefly. She has mother-worry eyes and eyebrows. Her mouth purses. She blinks. Long eyelashes on a blond are always beautiful. I quickly stare at the toilet-paper roll, then feel dumb, shift my gaze to the mirror. That way I can look at her without looking at her. "You can tell them to release the Sig," I go. "No one outside of my immediate family has done anything bad to me," I say. "I'm fine."

She closes her eyes. She sighs. Her sigh has years in it.

"Look," she says, and her voice is tired out. She rubs her temple. She opens her eyes. I'm still looking in the mirror to see her. She stands up. Her hair smell wafts between us. Goddamn it. It's the kind of hair smell that makes you want to bury your face in the waves.

"Too much has happened for me to try to change it. I mean you and me. You're all grown up." When she says "you and me" she waves her hand in the air between us like she's shooing away flies. When she says "you're all grown up" she puts her hands on her knees and spanks her kneecaps twice.

Something at the corner of my left eye aches.

She stares at her knees. "I blew it. I know it."

My throat squeezing.

"You know, when I was pregnant with you, I left your father."

Breath jacked. Lock-jawed. Wha-wha-whut?

"I mean I thought I would leave him." She looks up at me. "I came to this Holiday Inn. This room. I lay down on that bed," she points to the bathroom wall. On the other side Ave Maria is probably lying right where she did. "I drank an entire bottle of vodka, and I put an entire bottle of Xanax in my mouth. The television was on. I rested there like that for some time. Some of the Xanax dissolved and went down my throat. I put my hands on my gigantic bare belly. You were in there. You kicked."

She laughs that ironic kind of laugh people do when they don't believe what they just said and closes her eyes. "You kicked really hard. Hard enough so that I yelped. Like you were already wearing your Doc Martens. It was just so obvious you were pissed off at me." She laughs again. "I spit the pills out onto the floor. Then I slept."

If I have feet, I don't feel them. Or shins or knees. Even my hands and face feel like feathers. Still, I don't move my eyes off of the mirror. Even though they've gone all watery blur, I don't blink. I got no words for this. What sentence do you make when your mother just told you she tried to off herself with you waiting inside her belly for your ticket out?

"Dora, I want to tell you something important."

Really? Great timing.

"You aren't going to like it, but it will be true anyway."

Awesome.

"Dora, you're gonna have to learn to choose your battles. You have to stop fighting everything, and learn when to fight something that matters."

Part of me wants to punch her straight in the kisser. You've been NUMBO for seventeen years and NOW you want to deliver some sage advice? Like we're a mother and daughter? I clench my jaw and unclench it and clench it and unclench it. Wish I could put something in my mouth and bite the fuck out of it.

"'S that it?" I ask.

"Oh fuck it," she says. She stands up, turns away from me toward the shower curtain, then turns back. "It's just that," and she reaches into her back pocket and pulls out a piece of paper. "This is for you," she says, holding the piece of paper out to me. "It's why I went to Vienna. Somebody died. Somebody you never knew, but I did. At least for a while. My ... my mother."

For about thirty seconds I just let her hand and the piece of paper sit suspended in the air between us. A mother, a daughter, a piece of paper. It's the most large thing that's passed between us in a very long time. Maybe ever. On the other side of the wall Ave Maria is trying to match television commercial jingles with her voice. Finally I take the piece of paper.

You know what? It's not a piece of paper. It's a big bank check. Powder blue. A check for $1.7 million. You heard me. Made out to Ida Bauer. My birth name. Whoever she is.

Money. Again. Sig. Silverfuck. Now her. Is everything there is about being a girl in this world about money or genitals? Is life just a giant series of transactions?

My breathing goes weird. The check looks like a forgery. A cartoon. A graphic art project. A Xerox. A reproduction. Anything but real. I quickly crumple it up hard in my hand and pop it in my mouth. My mother doesn't flinch. I stare at her staring at me in the mirror. Inside my mouth the crumpled-up fortune tastes like wood pulp and ink. It fills my mouth and jabs at the flesh of my cheeks. I turn and look at my mother head on.

She tilts her head and crosses her arms over her boobs. She sighs. She has the hint of a smile. "She wanted you to have the silver set as well," my mother says, "but I suspect you'd just bend all the heads over or something equally … imaginative."

I can't help it. It makes me laugh. All those spoons with their heads bowed like dutiful fucked-up silver nuns. I reach down into my knee sock and pull out the spoon I nearly always have with me. Against my skin. I hold it up between us. On the convex side is my elongated spooky-looking head. On the concave side is hers. We both smile. Alike almost. Only my smile has paper where teeth should be, like when you put an orange peel there. I bend the head of the spoon over and hand it to her.

"I'll treasure it," she says, maybe kidding.

I turn back to the mirror. I spit the crumpled up $1.7 mil out of my mouth into the bathroom sink. I uncrumple it. I stare at it in the sink. It's damp, but salvageable. I don't mean the check just. I mean my life.

"Happy birthday, Dora," my mother says, as she almost seems to move toward me kinda like we might embrace.

Epiloguish Thingee

HOSPITALS. FUCK 'EM. I'VE HAD MY FILL, I CAN TELL YOU.

Same creepy fluorescent lighting, same odd assortment of losers waiting in earth-toned little hell rooms, same bizzaro industrial floor-cleaner smell mixed with sweat and blood. Flocks of fucky doctors and nurses milling about. Ave Maria is sitting across from me in a – you guessed it, Naugahyde chair – swinging her legs up and down. Little Teena is thumbing through an issue of *American Sailing*. I'm making my signature fingernail patterns in a Styrofoam coffee cup.

We're waiting for Marlene to come out of surgery. They won't let us anywhere closer because we're not family.

There's a lot I could tell you about that word family.

A month after the Holiday Inn episode me, Ave Maria, and Little Teena ate lunch in the restaurant on top of the Space Needle. Courtesy of Ave Maria's mom. All three of us high as kites, higher even than the Space Needle. Ave Maria pitched bites of food with a fork over her tipsy mother's head, Little Teena wore a fez, Obsidian ordered some dessert on fire and for the first time I noticed that the view up there? It's kind of awesome. If you walk around the thing in a circle, and you can avoid the freaky vertigo because of the slightly slanted walkway and the ever-so-slowly-spinning disk, it's downright gorgeous. The sound. The mountains. The city. All the neighborhoods and sigh and bulge of life.

I ordered lamb for lunch. I've never eaten lamb. I feel bad

for eating baby sheep but FUCK it's good. Like melt-in-your-mouth good. And after two martinis, who gives a shit about PETA? It was kind of a going-away party. Ave Maria is going to Yale. You heard me. What? I told you they were rich. I do wish I could plant a nanny cam in her room just to see how the snooty snoots react to her. Little Teena got a paid gig down in San Francisco to tickle the ivories at a gay jazz club. I know! Life is good.

About our … teen drama, well, I already told you: wigs work. No one ever had any idea who we were. Or are. There is no surveillance camera footage. No evidence we were ever there. Except some cockamamie story the three men who were arrested told.

The three stooges, AKA the publicity agent and his goons, were arrested for attempted kidnapping. Turns out Marlene was in the trunk of their car. When they ran out that night to chase us and discovered the Obsidian-slashed tires, Smiley called the cops from inside the halfway house and enunciated perfectly into the phone that three perpetrators who had killed the intake guy at the halfway house also had some big black tranny in the trunk of their car and they were trying to escape. "Murderous perverts," Ted kept saying into the phone. "Preying on helpless trapped children!" But when the cops arrived, Smiley just went back to his shtick.

There was no record of Obsidian ever having existed.

Someone in the hospital waiting room farts. I look at Little Teena. He nods his head up and down in the universal yup, 'twas I gesture, then says, "Why does everything about sailing sound like gay sex?" He looks up from his magazine. "Check it: able-bodied seaman. Aft bow spring line. Anchor ball. Anchor chocks. Barrelman. Back and fill. Bimini top. I mean christ, it sounds like some kind of SM play party."

Ave Maria laughs like a shy little girl and covers her face. Then she goes, "Whoa," solemnly. She holds her arms out in front of her. Her wrists have brown and yellow and blue bruises on them. Faint, but there. From me. "Aren't those the coolest bracelets in ever?"

I love her I love her I love her.

I look down at my dirtwater coffee cup. In spite of myself, I've carved a fingernail heart.

Obsidian and me, we're having an A-frame built in the woods near a crazy lesbo aunt she has who got booted off the reservation for constantly beating all the men at poker and making her own peyote-laced hooch. I don't mind telling you, that hooch is tasty. And whirly. We might expand that into a business.

I'd tell you where exactly but frankly I don't want to talk to people much for a while. It's near the Nisqually Wildlife Refuge though. Bats, rabbits, beavers, bears, foxes, coyotes, salmon, harbor seals, and all manner of birds ... I had no idea how cool animals were until I met them. The wingnut lesbo aunt – who isn't wingnut at all but we help her keep the story up – she gave me a present. It's a sealskin hat. It kind of looks like a union soldier hat only, you know, seal skin-y. She says the seal is my animal totem.

Animal totem, huh? I knew a guy once who told me all about totems ... what's your feeling about rats? Crazy lesbo aunt said they were sacred but gross. I said, well is there some kind of ritual or prayer thing I should do? Can I switch being from whitey space city and become part of your tribe? She looked at me like I was an idiot. "This isn't fucking *Dances with Wolves*, kimosabe, but it's a good hat in the rain," and she laughed, and I laughed, and Obsidian laughed, and we drank whirly wine and can I just say, laughing is cool.

As for my girl wall story, well, I remixed it and turned it into a bitchin' little art installation called "Dora: A Headcase." You have to enter a Dora room lined with pink plastic and vag fur and Vaseline in order to experience it. When you get inside, the walls are words. There are stories about everything that's happened to me in my dumb little life. There are lines from sex books and lines from bands and lines I collected in bathroom stalls all over the city. And letters to Francis Bacon and even advice here and there to Sig, like "Sig, you gotta decrease your douche-hood next time you get a girl client." On the ceiling of the girl room is a film with the most bitchin' soundscape you will ever hear in your life playing in a loop. The sounds of boots on pavement and wind and rain banging the cord of a flagpole. The sound of dog breath and Lexus engines and bum pee and violin concertos all mixed together. Ave Maria's high notes and things waitresses at Shari's yelled at us and falling glass. The sound of water. Of a metal bar rolling on the concrete of a parking garage. Birds and electricity hum. Sound is everywhere besides in your voice.

I won a buncha arty awards for it. Very cool.

The hospital waiting room smells like air freshener and hand sanitizer and plastic valves mixed with Little Teena's fart. Ave Maria stands up and says, "I'm going to sing a hospital sex-change song!"

Some old bag walks by right when she says that and makes a raisin-faced grimace at us.

"Bite me," I say. The old bag shuffles away like someone bit her ass.

"Good christ," Little Teena says, and goes back to his magazine.

Ave Maria paces in tiny circles with her eyes closed, humming to herself.

I reach inside my Dora purse and turn on my H4n. Little Teena rattles off sailing terms.

"Blue peter. Chafing gear. Chain locker. Cheeks."

I look at the digital time on my iPhone. Marlene's been in there three hours. There are basically three kinds of sex re-assignment procedures once you go through the years of therapy and cross-dressing necessary to complete a sex change. Marlene's been pre-op ready for quite a while, just saving up money.

The first type is called penile inversion vaginoplasty. That's where they turn the wang skin inside-out and use it to line a vag.

The second is called scrotal graft vaginoplasty. That's used when there's not enough wang skin to create the vag and vag lining, so they use scroti skin too. Apparently you get more wang depth this way.

The third is the sigmoid colon vaginoplasty. Pretty much what it looks like. They use part of your bunghole skin to help create vag. Kinda tougher skin. More … rubbery. But it has my favorite name.

In each case the surgeon constructs the labia majora, sensated labia minora, clitoral hood, and sensated clitoris.

You are looking at between ten and twenty-five grand.

Drop in the bucket when you've got $1.7 mil.

Ave Maria begins to sing. She's holding her fist up to her mouth in the classic air microphone way.

It's not an original, it's better. It's Velvet Underground. I turn the volume recorder up on the H4n in my purse. I hold my iPhone up and videotape her. She turns slowly in circles while she sings, eyes closed, her free hand pulling at her strings of hair.

"You missed your calling," Little Teena says. "You shoulda been in a band."

"Hell yeah," I say. "Daughters of Eve."

"Wicked," Ave Maria pipes. "Let's get T-shirts!"

I'll be your mirror.

Great fucking line. Seems so fucking … APT right this second. For Marlene. When she's out, we've got to bust ass to be good mirrors for her. But also for us. We gotta keep reflecting back to each other else get caught in this pop money death culture's gaze. We gotta make our own families and write our own sexualities our own selves. Story it.

Ave Maria pumps up the volume. Orderlies get curious and sniff near us. There's only one thing to do – I stand up and reach my hand out to Little Teena. He accepts my invitation. We dance. Like punks let loose.

Sing it, Ave Maria, sing it.

Because I Know
You Want to Know

YEAH, I SAW THE SIG.

Three times after that, to be exact.

The first time I went to see him was the day after the Holiday Inn meet. He was still being held for molestation and arson. Apparently it took a while for the paperwork to go through after my mother dropped the charges. So I spoke to him through Plexiglas at the Seattle jail. I picked up the black phone on my side, circa 1968. He picked up the black phone on his side.

"You look like shit," I said.

"You look positively radiant," he said. "You have hair. Sort of."

I ran my fingers through my crop of barely there hair. It did kind of feel like hair.

"You know I told them you are my doctor, right? I mean for real?"

He put his other hand on the desk in front of him and rapped his fingers like he was playing piano. Immediately I felt like a dumbass. "Am I supposed to thank you?" he said without looking at me.

We sat there like lumps with shitty black phones in our hands for a minute. Then I knocked on the window. He looked back up at me. "Can I ask you something?" I went.

"Certainly," he said.

"What are you gonna do with your rack of case studies?"

"I've not decided," he said quietly. Then, "My career has

careened as of late … I'll have to sort a few things out, if you know what I mean. I may leave the country."

"You got hot lawyers I bet," I went. Which seemed suddenly like an infantile thing to say. You got hot lawyers? After everything we'd been through that's what I said to him? I stared at him. I could see the blue veins at his temples and on the tops of his hands. His eyes pocketed inside folds of flesh and lines. I don't know why I never noticed before, but his ears are enormous and saggy. Also old-man ear hair is jutting out.

Goddamn it. I can't remember what the fight was about. Why'd I fight him? He looked like somebody's grandpa – in sad little orange pajamas.

It was a draw of sorts. An old man behind Plexiglas in orange pajamas. A young woman with a vag bag.

"I just want my stories to be mine," I went, holding up my Dora purse. Why'd I even say that?

The Sig coughed. Then he coughed a lot. But he kept the phone at his ear.

"I hear that coughing is a diversion tactic," I said, smiling like ha ha jokey.

Sig coughed some more, then smiled, then just looked like the saddest old man balls in the universe, then he hung up the phone.

"Bye then," I went.

And that was that.

The next time I saw him I was thirty.

To be honest with you, he didn't look all that much older than he did behind the Plexiglas. He had his old man on but more neatly trimmed. And smaller and thinner. Like a shrinking Sig. I saw him in his office, if you can believe it. He made me tea. He asked me politely about my life, so I told him Obsidian and I had started our own vineyard and were producing organic pinot. That we hoped to build an artist colony for girls with a bunch more A-frames. I told him I built a small filmmaking studio to the side of our home. Everything seemed to please him. He seemed calm and gentle, though each time he raised his teacup to his mouth, his hand tremored quite noticeably.

At one point he produced a cigar from his jacket pocket, and so I stood up and crossed over to him and lit it for him. Between puffs of smoke he said, "So kind." His cigar? It just looked like a cigar.

We talked about my story. About how my father had betrayed me, how my mother had neglected me, how I needed to pass through a psychosexual crucible of sorts to work things through. The sentences seemed effortless and without drama.

"Thank you for believing me," I remember saying to him. "I think it was important, that you never called me a liar," I said.

"Your lies located themselves in deeper places. No doubt part of the reason you are an artist," he said. "Though I always felt our time together had resulted in …"

I waited.

"Failure," he said. "On my part."

I stood up and moved toward him and opened my mouth to protest or something but he put his hand up between us like a five-fingered stop sign. And anyway, what would I have said? Done? I sat back down.

When the top of the hour of the visit came, his old cuckoo clock erupted, and to my surprise and delight, a cuckoo came shooting out. We laughed.

"My cuckoo is mended!" he announced, and we laughed more, but I suddenly saw that in spite of his age he looked exactly like a wizened child, nearly engulfed by his camel-back chair, cigar smoke giving him a dream-like elfin quality.

I never made the film of his phallic adventure. The footage is archived, stored in several different forms in my studio. Sometimes I watch it like other people might watch home movies, and I smile. It's not mockery. It's nostalgia. For a drama that was a girl.

The third time was at his gravesite. In Vienna. Obsidian and I were visiting my mother in Europe. I'd heard that he had died there from her. His collected case studies were being compiled and a wing of the library would be dedicated to his life's work. Beautifully archived and taken care of like the work of Franz Schubert.

Sigmund Freud smoked about twenty cigars a day all his adult life. He developed malignant oral cancer, but hid it for years. He underwent nearly thirty surgeries. The rest is all just a story passed like gossip between doctors, but the story goes that a well-known fellow doctor assisted him in suicide. That he wanted to die inside imagination, inside the act of reading literature, that the last book he read was a novel by Balzac. That his doctor friend pumped him with enough morphine to drop a horse, until he died inside a lovely, dizzy, exquisite interpretation of a roman à clef.

I know what Sig would say. He'd say we live out classic family romances, and there's no way around it. On the other hand, goddamn it, is everything in life really all that fucking oedipal?

Because if it is, you know, just shoot me.

Acknowledgements

RHONDA HUGHES REMAINS A LITERARY HEROINE TO ME for her bravery and integrity; no better collaboration between writer and editor/publisher exists. Anywhere. Here it is straight-no-chaser: this book would not exist without the help of the posse. So: thank you Chuck Palahniuk for the idea about you know what and that other thing and especially the part that is going to creep out everyone but you and me. And for laughing. Thank you Monica Drake for already being as nerd-girl obsessed with Dora and Freud as I was. Thank you Chelsea Cain for liking Ave Maria – parts of her I made pretending you and me grew up best friends. And for the title. Thank you Suzy Vitello for "getting" the psychology stuff and the Gemini stuff and forgiving me for being the daughter I probably was and liking me anyway. Thank you Erin Leonard for writing weird things that make the weird things I write seem less foreign. Thank you Cheryl Strayed for loving those mother and father pages we both know I made up from a deep wishful place. Thank you Diana Page Jordan for understanding how big a deal it is to survive and then tell about it through stories. Thank you Mary Wysong-Haeri for the secrets we passed back and forth and the sneaker wine dates. And thank you to the Mingo, who read every damn word, every page, and told me how to better kick ass before I brought them to the posse. All quotes from Sigmund Freud from *Dora: An Analysis of a Case of Hysteria* (Touchstone, 1997).